AUSTIN·1980

ANDRE NORTON
VOORLOPER

Illustrated by Alicia Austin

1.

The Shadow Death struck Mungo Town just after harvest, as if it had purposefully waited to give the greatest pain, the harshest of deaths. Perhaps there *was* a method in that time selection. What can an off-worlder know of a new colony's lurking dangers in spite of all the assurances from Survey testers that another planet is waiting free and open to settlers? No one knew of Voor's menace until the fiftieth year after first-ship landing, and then it was only a handful of outpost villages and holdings which were hit and the reasons given were practical and believable.

Bad water, contaminated food, attacks of heretofore unknown dangerous animals—you can read these explanations all in the official files if you have a morbid interest in how part of a new colony began to die. The next year it was worse. Then death came to Voor's Grove a few days after the planting. There were four survivors—two infants, one three-year-old girl, and a woman who never gave coherent answers to questions, but crooned unendingly to herself, until one night she managed to elude containment at the medic's center and disappeared. They tracked her as far as the edge of the Tangle and that was that. Once in the Tangle anyone must be written off.

So it was on Voor. But colonists are a tough lot and people who are crowded off one of the League's Chain Worlds do not have much choice, after all. There were two whole years after the Grove strike when there was no trouble at all. People do forget—even after they have gone through the rigorous pre-settlement training. There were always the preferable believable excuses, as I have said.

Those did not hold after Mungo. You can wipe out twenty or so people, but when the death toll comes to two hundred and twenty—it is not that easy to find logical explanations.

That was how I came to be a Voorloper. I grew up in a trek wagon and could inspan the gar team before I could heft a shoulder weight of trade goods. I was second generation from first-ship. First-ship people always have a certain standing on any colonial world. They were those willing to gamble the most, and usually they end up either dead or prosperous enough to carve out their own holdings and make them pay. On most worlds that is true. On Voor those who survived became lopers—they knew the score.

My mother died at Mungo's Town and my father, Mac Turley s'Ban, after he returned to find the ruin there, inspanned his smartest gars, loaded his treker, threw me in on top of what he believed would best suit a loper's needs, and took off. I was about six then and now I can't even remember what it is like to live rooted and not as a loper. There are still holdings, but they don't push out northward any more—mostly they

©AUSTIN-1980

stick to the southern portion of the big land, on that side of the Halb Canyon river. The north has some settlements—mostly miners after Quillian Clusters. Those keep up forcefields at night, and that solution is too expensive a drain on any ag-man's credits. For some reason none of the brains the League has sent can understand why the Shadow doesn't spread south. For the last few years they have not sent out any "experts on X-Tee" any more. We aren't rich enough a world to pull such help. Our potential, my father once said, would not pay off fast enough.

He always had that set to his jaw whenever he met a League man. In fact I've known him to sit lock-toothed all evening when a couple rode into our camp and tried to question him. He would even get up and disappear into the wagon and leave them there with their mouths half open, looking as slack brained as a goof-monkey. After a while he got a reputation and even a holdings man never mentioned Shadows when he was around.

I don't know what he'd done before he earthed in on Voor in the beginning. He never talked about the old days, just as he never mentioned my mother. Once or twice, when I got old enough to really notice things, I wondered if he had been enlisted in Survey himself. He seemed to have a lot of strange scraps of learning about treking. Then from the first he made notes on a recorder. In fact the only off-world thing he ever got for himself (except stunner shells) when we went Port Side once a year for our stock was a case of tapes.

Though some of those were for me. Even though we were on the move all the time, he saw that I was not dirt stupid. I had to learn, and I will say this, I really liked it. First it was all practical stuff—filling in what he didn't show me. He listened to that, too. I learned to repair a stunner, a food synthesizer, a hand com. We did jobs like that at holdings now and then.

Then there was history—of the League, and of several different worlds. I never understood why he picked those special ones and I knew better than to ask. They were a queer mixture—no two alike, and none near Voor as far as I could tell—at first. Later I began to see what they did have in common—Astra, and Arzor, and Kerdam, Slotgoth—they had all begun as Ag worlds—just like Voor. Only it turned out later that they had a lot of Forerunner remains on them—and some queer things had happened there as a result.

I was not too good with the tech tapes. It took me a long time to become as competent a craftsman as my father demanded. He had a lot of patience, and it was as if he was making very sure that I was going to be able to use my hands well enough to make me a good living before he was through with me. I did learn, too. But I was better with animals. I could handle the gars, as I have said, when I was too little to climb onto one. Somehow they liked me—or else I had that kind of a gift—

My father talked sometimes about natural gifts. He made sure that I understood men were not all alike. Of course, I don't mean just aliens and Terrans (*that* any

one with a tenth of a brain in his head already knew) but men—Terrans themselves—had different talents they used—when they knew how. Once he started to talk about Psi, then shut up quick and got that locked look on his face. It had been healing he had been explaining to me then. I wished he'd go on—but he never mentioned that again.

There were the healers. Mostly they were girls or young women. I had seen them do some things in the out-back which were not explained on any tape. My father appeared to dislike them, or else there was something about their talents he distrusted. He was always uneasy when one of them was anywhere near him. Once I saw him deliberately turn and walk away when a healer at Jonas Holding was going to speak to him.

She was a nice looking young woman radiating a kind of peaceful feeling. Even being near a healer could make a person feel warm and comfortable inside. I saw her stand and look after my father and there was a sad look on her face. She even half raised her hand as if to lay a healer's touch on something which was not there at all.

However there were other gifts my father did discuss —such as psychometry, where you could hold something in your two hands and tell through your own feelings about it who had made it—where it came from. Then there was foreseeing—though my father said that was rare and not always to be trusted. There were some people, too, who could read thoughts—tell what a person was thinking—though he had never met anyone like that—just knew about them from tapes, and things he had seen once or twice.

Aliens had a lot of such powers, but they did not always work between Terran-human and them. Our brains were too different for that. Though sometimes those aliens who were the farthest from us in body structure seemed closest in mind.

My father would never use any weapon stronger than a stunner, and he never had a blazer in the wagon. He was strong about that—but he made me a good marksman with both stunner and tangler. We did have times when we needed those. I had a sand cat charge me once and its foreclaws dug gouges out of the earth about a finger's length from my boot toes when I brought it down. We just left it sleeping there. My father never killed for pelts the way some lopers did. He was very firm about that even when the Portsiders wanted him to bring in jaz fur and he knew right well where a colony of jaz nested. It was not because jaz were too easy to kill—a jaz at nesting time was something a wise loper kept away from. They hunted men with a cunning which made them a nasty kind of danger if you got up among the Spurs.

Yes, my father gave me an odd education—both by tape and by example. He had a different rep among the other lopers, too. About every two years or so, he deliberately crossed the Halb, he said to visit the mines. We did trade with one or two. But I got to know early that was not the main reason we took a chance most lopers did not care for—in spite of the mine transport paying off so well.

Because we never headed straight for the mine territory. Instead we'd circle around, always stretching on each trip a little farther north. Then we'd visit dead holdings. Though my father told me early we were never to mention that. At first he would go in among the deserted buildings alone; he'd even suit up—he had a full Survey suit such as they wore on the first-in trips on other planets. He always ordered me to stay back at the trek wagon with the com. It was also his order that if he did not report every so many time units I was to inspan and get the hell out as fast as I could make it, making me swear on the Faith of Fortune I wouldn't try to come in after him.

My father was a true-believer and he raised me so. At least I was believer enough to know that you did not break that oath—ever—that a man's own faith in himself would rot and fade away if he ever did.

After a while he did not suit up if the holding was one he had visited before, but he still did if it was a new one. When he came back he would dictate into a tape just what he had noticed—even the smallest things—such as what kind of weeds were growing now in the old gardens, and whether anything had been looted out of the houses—nothing ever was. The strangest thing was that there were never any animals or birds to be found anywhere near a holding which had been cleared out by the Shadows. But vegetation always grew very rankly there. Not the imported food stuffs which had been specially conditioned for planting on Voor, but weird things which were not even of the native Voor growth we knew. My father did drawings of that—only he wasn't too skilled at the job; but he described it carefully, though he never brought back any specimens.

After every such visit he did something else which would have made any Portside official think he was ready for reconditioning. He would make me tie him

15

up, wrists and feet, and put him into a sealed sleep bag. I was to keep him so for a day and a night. Again he made me swear that if he started to talk funny or fought to get loose I was to inspan and get out—leave him there there all fastened down and not come back for maybe two, three days. I had to swear I would because he was so demanding about it. Though I think I would have risked breaking *that* oath if I had ever had to. Luckily it never happened like he feared.

I knew what he searched for—though we never discussed it—some answer to the riddle of the Shadow doom. It was not for the benefit of Voor at large, but because he had within him a burning desire to bring to justice, if such a thing were possible, that which had ended his stable life.

Voorlopers are solitary men. A number, like my father, were refugees from blasted northern holdings who had survived because they were away when the doom struck. Others were misfits, loners, men who could not root themselves in any place, but were ever wandering in search of something which perhaps even they could never understand. They talked very little, their long stretches of lonely travel taking from them much of the power to communicate with their fellows, except over such elemental things as trade.

If one chanced upon a holding at the harvest festival he might linger, watching the festivities with a detached wonder, as one might view the rites of an alien people.

There were several who traveled in pairs but my father and I were the only two of close kinship I had knowledge of. They had no women. If they assuaged a natural hunger of the body it might be in one of the

Portcity pleasure houses (even on such an undeveloped world as Voor a few of these existed, mainly for the patronage of the ship's crews). However, no woman ever rode in a trek wagon.

Women are jealousy guarded on Voor as they are on most frontier planets. The ratio is perhaps one female to three males, for pioneer life did not generally appeal to unwed women. Those who came were already hand-fasted to some man. Remarriage came quickly to widows, and daughters were prized, even more than sons, since a man might tie to his holding some highly desirable male help could he provide a wife for one of the unattached.

Only the healers came and went freely. Their very natures were their safeguards and they were valued so highly that, had any man raised his eyes to one covetously, he would have signed his own warrant for outlawry and quick death thereafter. Healers did wed when their powers began to wane, for those powers were at their strongest from the beginning of adolescence until they were in their third decade. Then they had their pick of husbands, for there was every hope that any daughter of such a union might inherit the gift.

We were at trade in the northmost of the holdings—Ratterslea—and I had then grown to match my father in inches, though I was still not his match in strength, when I first heard directly of my mother. I had taken a packet of thread and needles (a favored betrothal gift on Voor) to the Headhouse where Ratter's wife received me in guest style, the tankard of fall ale and the bread-of-traveler set out on a tray she held herself, rather to my surprise, for I was no son of any holder, nor an off-worlder.

She was tall, and in her hip-length smock of bright cloth with its many bands of embroidery to show off her skill, her breeches and boots of well-tanned gar hide, smooth as the thread I had to offer, she made a fine figure of a woman. Her hair was the color of darth leaves when the first breath of frost wind touches them —ruddy and yet gold—and it was bound about her head like those bands of ceremony worn on other worlds by great rulers—those they term "crowns".

In her sun-browned face her eyes were a strange, vivid green and they were eyes which searched and probed, so that I, who seldom said even a word to any woman, felt very ill at ease and wondered if I had in truth washed all the road dust from me before I had dared to come.

"Greeting, Bart s'Lorn." Her voice was rich and deep as the shade of her hair.

I was a little startled at her words for though I was very used to being called "Bart", yet this was the first time in my memory that I had been also greeted by my full clan-family name. "s'Lorn" was strange to me—it was the first time I had heard the reference to my long dead mother.

"Lady of the Holding," I produced my best guest courtesy, "may fortune smile upon this rooftree and your daughters be as handmaidens to that fortune. I have that which you have ordered and it is our wish that it find favor with you—"

I held out the packet but she did not look to it. Rather still she studied me and I grew yet more uneasy and even wary, though I was sure that in no way could I have offended her or any under her roof.

"Bart s'Lorn," she repeated the name and there was something in the tone of her voice which I was stranger to. "You are very like—male though you are. Eat, drink, bless so this house—"

I was yet further amazed, for such a greeting is given only to a close kinsman, one who is esteemed and very welcome in either good times or bad. Since she did not take the packet from me, I placed it on a nearby table and did as she bade, even as if I had been a youngling of her own household and not near a man grown. Carefully I broke the bread-of-the-traveler into two portions. One I dipped within the tankard, end down. Though at that moment my mouth seemed dry and I was indeed far from hunger, I put the moistened portion between my lips. Steadying the tray with one capable hand, my hostess did the same with the other piece of the thin round, thus sharing food in ceremony with me.

"Yes," she said slowly when she had swallowed that traditional mouthful, "you have very much the look of her, Voor born though you are."

That bite of moistened bread which I had taken seemed to stick within my throat. I gulped it down hastily.

"Lady of the Holding, you speak of s'Lorn—that name my mother bore." There were questions in plenty pushing into my mind and as yet I could not sort out which were of the greatest importance. At that moment it rushed upon me how much I had always longed to know of the past and yet had never dared to ask of my father.

"Sister's sister she was to me." The relationship my hostess claimed was one by marriage. In some clan holdings it was as close as that of shared bloodkin. "My sister was Hagar Lorn s'Brim, and her sister— she pledged to Mac Turley s'Ban."

I bowed. "Lady, forgive my ignorance—"

"Which is none of your fault," she countered briskly. "All men and women know of that which came to Mac Turley s'Ban and what a wound it gave him, which has not healed even to this day. Did he not send you here, not coming himself, for he will have no speech or meeting with those who once knew him in happiness and full strength of clan." She shook her head slightly.

"He has made of you a holdless, kinless one. Does this ride hard on you?" Again I met her eyes and felt that measure of being weighed and searched, as if she would have each thought and feeling out of me, plain before her as a reading tape is spread.

It was my turn to stand straight and proud. Holdless and kinless I might be in her eyes, but in my own I had a place I knew at that moment I would not trade for all the land and gear which made up the wealth this prosperous holding displayed with pride.

"I am a voorloper, lady. My father has, I think, no reason to find me less than he wishes—"

"And *you* wish?"

"Lady, I think that I could never be other than I am."

"Well, it is true that a gar trained to the hunt cannot be harnessed to the plow—else the spirit be broke. Also perhaps the Shadow has touched also on you—"

"The Shadow!" Even here below the Halb that word had an evil ring.

"There are shadows and Shadows," she returned. "Enter, Bart s'Lorn, now that we have met at last, let me know more of you."

She ushered me through the great hall where there were many about their tasks: a girl at the loom, another carding the fleecy hair of those small gars which are bred for their coats, older women busy at oven and open stove. They all looked at me with frank curiosity and appraisal and I put on an outward show of what

23

I hoped equaled my father's habitual aloofness. Though I marked one girl who sat on a chair, not a stool, before the fire and who did not look at me at all, rather gazed as one who could see beyond wall and room, dreaming with open eyes. Her hands were idle and lay limp, palm up upon her knees, and her upper smock was of dull green, shorter than those generally worn, more akin to the riding dress of a traveler.

She we passed and came into the far end of the room where there were two cushioned chairs. On one of those my hostess seated herself, waving me to the other. Straightway she began questioning me and such was the authority in her voice I found myself answering, not through polite courtesy, resenting inwardly that any so attempt to enter my life, but rather as if indeed she *were* bloodkin and had such a concern for me that she had a right to know such things.

Though the holding was far from Portcity, she was plainly one well learned in many things and with a taste for some of the same ways of life my father honored. She had questions concerning him also, where we went and what we did.

At first I tried to evade her directness, thinking that our concerns were none of hers in truth. Then she spoke to me emphatically:

"He would not have so sent you to me, *me* of all this world, had he not wanted me to know this, Bart. For he understands from the old days what manner of person I am and what moves in me, even as it has made of him a rootless, roofless man. For I, too, was at Mungo's Town—though I was also gone when the Shadows came."

In all the ways she had surprised me since our meet-

ing, this gave me the greatest stroke of amazement. I had not known in all my years any others who had lived in that ill-omened place.

"Shadow dead—all of them—" her face grew then near as grim as my father's could upon occasion, rounder of cheek and chin though it might be. "You alone—why—"

"Not, I alone—there was my father!" I corrected her.

She shook her head. "He was on journey that night, he came back. You lay in the bed—not crying—rather as if you slept though your eyes were open. It has happened elsewhere. Always it is a child who lives—or sometimes an elder whose memory does not thereafter

25

return. Tell me, what can you remember—the farthest back of all memories!"

Her demand was sharp. It was one my father had never made, perhaps because he did not want—or dare—to do so. That he had been away from the town when the Death had come—that much I had always known.

What did I remember? Had she not so caught me perhaps I would not have automatically obeyed her command and tried to recall my first clear memory. I had heard men, and women, too, boast that they remember this or that happening which reached back to the time when they crawled on all fours or were carried in arms. What did I remember?

With real effort I closed my eyes, for to me memory most often presents itself in pictures as if I were running through some reading tape of my own devising. What then did I see?

There was a hot sun blazing over my head, I could feel it even as the ground swayed, far down and away, for I was perched on the wide back of an animal which ambled peacefully along, snatching, as it went, mouthfuls of leafy brush which was high enough on either hand so it could so graze without bending its head to the ground. My two hands grasped tightly the stubby mane of the gar as I stared about at its horns. It was a wagon beast and was yoked to a fellow that also mouthed at leaf and stick with flabby, mobile lips.

There was the yoke before me, such a yoke as I have handled many times since. So I rode in the sun and yet though I could feel the heat of that upon my head and shoulders, still I was cold, I shivered. And I was afraid. Yet what I feared so—no, my mind flinched from remembering. I could not recall.

A man came up beside the gar, a man so tall that even that great beast did not make him seem either small or lacking in strength. He swept me from my perch as if he knew that the fear was eating at me, held me to him, so that my head lay on his shoulder and my face in hiding against his body. I clung to him with desperation.

Though now I forced, and searched, and strove for the first time I could truly remember to recall the past, that was my first memory. I was five planet years old, on my first trek. Behind that—lay nothing.

I was not even aware that I must have been repeating aloud the description of the picture in my mind until I heard the woman near me catch her breath.

"Nothing farther back? Nothing of—of her?"

Did I begin to shiver again? I was not sure. Suddenly there was someone standing beside me on the other side, and a tankard was pressed into a hand which I found I had lifted as if to ward off some blow.

"Drink," said a soft voice and I sensed that special calming which is the healer's heritage.

I raised the tankard and drank, but first, over its rim, I looked at the one who had brought it to me. It was the girl of the green smock, she who had sat by the fire dreaming, or seeming to dream, and who alone in that hall had, as I believed, never seen me. Now she watched me alertly as the liquid she had brought me filled my mouth and I swallowed.

Was it sweet, or tart? Surely it was not of any ordinary brewing. I thought that somehow the taste of sunripened berries, of autumn ripe fruit, as well as the sharp freshness of spring water had all been caught in it, mixed with a subtlety to leave no one flavor or taste in full command. It was cool and yet it warmed. I forgot that cold which had begun to form an icy core within me. No, not forgot it perhaps, just knew that it no longer mattered, had been pushed far off so that it concerned someone else but not the me who was important, alive, and here and now.

"You are a healer," I stumbled awkwardly, stating the obvious.

"I am Illo." She added no clan or house ending to that single name. Some healers did indeed acknowledge no roof, no holding. Those were wanderers, serving those in need from place to place—in their own way like the lopers—yet far more involved with their fellows than we in that they cared deeply for strangers, whereas we stood aloof and could not summon such emotions even if we wished.

"She is also shadow touched," said my kinswoman. "Have you heard of Voor's Grove?"

All the Shadow tales were known to the lopers. "You were the girl then?" I said to her directly.

"Drink first," she bade me, nor did she answer until I had indeed finished to the last drop what brew filled the tankard and turned it upside down in the fashion of a feaster after a toast, to show that I had honored the words spoken.

"Yes," she said then as she held out her hand for the empty tankard. "I was of Voor's Grove, the first holding to be set in the north plains, planted and raised by Helman Voor, for whom this world was named. It may be even that I am of his blood kin," she shrugged. "Who knows? I do not remember—I cannot remember. I am Shadow touched."

2.

If I flinched again it was inwardly, for I held tightly to that outward calm which I patterned after my father's way of facing the problems of this world. Instead I asked now, with a boldness for which I was proud:

"What really is Shadow touch? Of all on this world a healer must best know the anser of that."

She wore a considering look on her face. Not, I thought, as if she were weighing whether she might trust me with any true answer, but because she was seeking to choose words which could explain something very difficult to make clear. Then she questioned in turn:

"What are the Shadows?"

Only it seemed that she did not expect any meaningful reply from me, for then she added:

"Until we learn that—then how can we also open the door in here," she touched forefinger to her broad forehead, uncovered, for she wore her hair fastened tightly back as most healers do, "where must lie the explanation for this curse."

Beside the lady of the holding she was slight, though tall. Her body was as spare as the lead wand of a loper, and had nothing about it of the ripeness of a woman bred to mother a child. Her skin was browned near dark as mine by sun and weather, and her features were a little sharp, their angularity made more apparent by the gauntness of her cheeks. Still she carried the calm and authority of her talent in her, so in her own way she was good rival to her hostess, for I did not believe that she was rooted here.

Now she looked at me directly again.

"There comes a need—"

I could make little sense of that and, when I would have asked her what she meant, she had turned swiftly and went back down the hall taking the tankard I had emptied with her. Now I glanced at my hostess.

Between her eyes a frown line deepened. She stared after the girl a long moment before she brought her eyes back to me once again.

"Where does Mac trek this season?" she asked abruptly.

"We go to Dengungha." I named the mine settlement he had sought out on the map before we left Portcity. It was the farthest north now of any settlement, closest to the waste of the Tangle. Beyond it lay only ruins—the ruins of Voor, of Mungo—neither of which we had ever visited during our wanderings. Our trek wagon carried some offworld equipment for the mine—a small cargo, one which would barely pay for our supplies. I had thought it strange that we shipped so little, but my father offered no explanation, and he was not one to be questioned unless there was definite reason.

"Dangungha," she repeated. "Then where—?"

I shrugged. "My father is trek master, his the trail plan."

Her frown had grown deeper. "I do not like it—there is—but it is true that one does not question Mac's coming—or going—one never did. He is a man to keep his own council. Only one ever could speak freely with him—"

I thought I could guess—

"My mother?"

"Yes. We thought him a dour, secretive man. Only when he was with her it was as if he threw away all defenses and came fully alive. You would not have known him, seeing him as he is today. She was his light—and much of his life. He is Shadow touched now, even if he himself never came under the curse in body or mind. I wish—" her voice trailed away into nothingness and I sat in courteous silence, though I began to wish that I were free of this hall. For to me it seemed like a cage, pressing in upon me.

There was the good smell of fresh bread, of other things which meant a well-run household. But such caught in my throat as if I smothered in them. I wanted the outside where there was no hum of talk, no clatter of loom, of pans, no bustle of work strange to me.

My hostess roused from her thoughts. "There is no reasoning with him. That we learned years since. He will go his own way, though to take you with him—"

Now a spark of heat flared in me. "Lady, I want nothing more than to be my father's son."

Once more she looked into my eyes and there was a sternness in her face as she answered me:

"Only a fool would say that was—is—not so. You must go your way in spite of all. The Faith of Fortune," between us she sketched in the air the sign of a blessing, "be with you Bart s'Lorn. You need the best that fair-wishing can bring you. We shall say your name before the Hearth Candle here each night."

I bowed my head and indeed she moved me with that solemn promise. I, who had no roots, nor had ever wanted them, did not know until that moment what it might mean to be so treated, as if indeed I were blood-kin with those ready to stand at my side, or at my back, were evil to rise in my path.

"Lady, I give you the thanks of the heart," I fumbled with courtesy words I had never had reason to use before. "It is a very kindly thing you do."

"Little enough." That set sternness was still in her face. "Little enough, for there is no turn in a chosen road. Give to Mac my good-wishing also, if he will take it, or if he ever thinks of the past which once was. He is— No, I shall not say such words to you. I do him no wrong in my thoughts, only I hold for him a very great pity."

She arose then and I got to my feet as swiftly, sensing that she would dismiss me. Still she walked again by my side down the hall and saw me through the door with full guest honor. I did not look back after the farewell words were said between us, for, oddly enough, I still felt uneasy and afraid. Not as I had when we had spoken of the Shadow—that was a thing which all men found ill to discuss—but rather I feared the hall itself and the abundant life there, a strange and alien life which in some way was vaguely threatening to my own.

My father had not chosen to outspan in the visitor's field, but had camped down by the river, some distance from the holding buildings. I had started down the footpath which led to the water and so on to our wagon when someone came from behind to match step with me.

I glanced up startled, for I had been deep in my thoughts. It was Illo, the healer, and her stride was free and near as long as mine, that of a traveler who had been on many trails in the past. There was a pack resting against her shoulders, a weather cloak folded and strapped to the top of that. She wore the thick-soled boots of a tramper, and in one hand was her healer's staff, a straight cutting of qui wood which had been peeled and smoothed so that it seemed to shine in the sunlight as if it were a rod of pure brilliance such as lit Portcity buildings.

"How can I serve you?" I asked quickly, for healers never come to any one save for a purpose. They do not walk idly, nor do they seek out conversation save when they have something meaningful to impart.

"You travel north. So do I go also. My way is long, and—" now she returned my glance, "perhaps there is little time. The truth being I would ask passage with you."

Such a temporary arrangement between loper and healer was not unknown, usually when, as Illo said now, there was a need for speed on a long trip. But the miners at Dengungha were all off-world men and they clung always stubbornly to a belief in their own medics. There would be no call for a healer to seek them out.

"I do not seek the mines—" She was not reading my

thought, of course. It must be well known by now where we would travel once we had crossed river. "There is another place."

Illo did not name it, and it was not courtesy to ask. Though I could not recall any holding now to the north—unless some party had gathered more courage to front the unknown during the months just behind us, and trailed into the forbidden land for a ground-breaking.

However, though a healer had the right to ask passage, I could not see that my father would take kindly to this addition to our party. Yet there was no refusal he could give and not offend all custom. She said nothing more, only walked beside me to our camp.

My father sat on his heels beside the fire. Close to his hand lay a pipe and from it trailed still a small thread of smoke. He had been indulging himself in his one great extravagance, for the dried stuff he smoked was from off-world and could only be obtained by near ruinous bargaining with some shipsman. What he took in such trades from time to time he guarded so well and used so seldom that a small pouch of it would last him for many months. Also he used it only, I had come to know, when he was low in spirit, or else under that dark cloud which made him, sometimes for days, even more silent and aloof.

He had a reader out and there was a coil of tape set in it. But he was not using it, rather looking into the fire as if whatever message he would know was better found there.

A loper learns quickly certain measures for protection. Our hearing, I am sure, is better than that of any who are holding born, or off-worlder. Though both my new companion and I wore the soft, many-fold soled boots which favored the feet of those who traveled, yet he became aware of us and glanced up.

That his mood was no good one I could see at once.
The frown which he turned upon Illo was dark. He got
slowly to his feet, a little stiffly, but standing as

straight as her staff should she set it pole-like in the earth.

"Lady—" even that word as he said it had the grating sound of some tool seldom used, even a little rust bound in a setting.

"I am Illo," she said. The healers never used honor words by choice. "I would travel beyond the river," she came directly to the point.

My father's frown grew darker and now he looked to me in accusation. I knew that it was in his mind then that I had, without reference to him, made some promise to this girl. Only again she must have understood at once.

"There have been no promises made to me," she said coolly. Nor did she glance to me. "You are trekmaster, so I say to you—I have need to go beyond the river."

"Why?" my father asked starkly and boldly. "There are no holdings there—now—"

"And the miners have their medics?" she completed his thought almost before that "now" was out from between his lips. "It is true, Trekmaster. Still—there is a need for me to go beyond the river. And—since there are no holdings, I come to you. All men know that Mac s'Ban alone travels there."

"The land is cursed." There was no friendliness in him, even though that inner peace which the healers cast (perhaps without willing it, merely because they are what they are) must be touching him as it was me. It would appear that his stubbornness was proof even against that.

"All men know that also—even the off-worlders," she agreed. "Do they not put force fields about where they hack and despoil the earth? Yet I say and mean it—there is a need for me in the north."

No man on Voor could stand against such a statement. A healer could sense the need for her services, and, having once had that call, there was nothing save her own hurt or death which could hold her back from answering it. Nor would any man stand against the compulsion which moved her when she so would journey. My father might hate to give her wagon room because of those dark depths and sorrows within him, but he could not say her no.

We broke camp with the dawn. My father had not asked me anything concerning my talk with the Lady of the holding, nor had I volunteered even her greetings, for the fact that we were three in camp instead of two made him as unapproachable as if there was about *him* a forcefield. Maybe there was—one of his will.

The gars came to the yoking at my whistle as I had long since trained them to do. They never wandered far in their grazing and lopers often said that we had the best-trained animals on the plains. There were six of them, prime beasts, for we tended them many times better than we treated ourselves. Against the brittle, sun-dried grass of the land their dusky blue-gray hides were plain to see. And they were beginning to grow the heavier coats of winter wool.

As we did not use them for holding tasks my father had never allowed their horns to be blunted, for there were beasts abroad eager enough to taste gar meat, and he insisted they must be able to defend themselves. There were three bulls, massive creatures with a wide curl of horn, two sprouting from above their eyes, the third and sharpest from the nose. The other

three were their mates, for the gars, like the human kind on most worlds, were monogamous, and also they mated for life. It was well known that a gar whose mate was slain or died of some accident often grieved and would not graze until it, too, wasted away.

Our wagon was port built under my father's orders and design, much of it finished by his hands and mine, and less than two years old now. It was of bals wood which, cut green, can be shaped—then, when dried under the sun for the right number of days, becomes metal-hard. Such could stand years of heavy use and yet not show scratch nor dent.

It was divided into sections, two for cargo—one small, one for that of bulk—while the front and third portion could serve as a home in storm time. Though most lopers have an ingrown desire to sleep in a bag under the trekwagons themselves when it can be done. We do not like walls, as I have said.

The river crossing was a ford, easy enough to make at this time of the year, since only the spring rains brought it high and fast enough to offer any mishap. On the far side there was a faint trace of road but my father turned from that and struck out across the width of the land itself.

If one were a bird or one of the fluttersnakes from the Tangle—one could perhaps have seen more than just a very distant blue shadow in the far distance. We lopers did not travel by set trail or roads in this part of the continent—if any other lopers ever took to the north except my father and I. There was a com receiver in the wagon which could set up an automatic guide to Dengungha but it was apparent my father was not going to depend upon that now.

I waited, as I walked beside our lead gars, for some question or even direction from Illo. However she paced steadily at our long learned stride—or near its equivalent—with no more words than my father had to offer.

Gars for all their bulk can even run should the situation demand such effort from them. The stampede of a wild gar clan is no safe thing. However their usual procedure is a steady trot which a man can match without undue effort, if he is trained to it. Our beasts always kept to that in the north, unless brought to a halt at order. It was as if they neither liked the land nor trusted it no more than we did and so preferred to keep in motion. Whereas in the south they often slowed to catch up mouthfuls of any brush or tall growing grass to munch wetly and noisily as they went.

We veered west steadily, though I knew well enough that the mine lay due north, and westward there could be nothing at all save one evil tongue of the Tangle which licked out into the plains, forming a curve as if to entrap therein any foolish enough to venture so near to its vile mass.

Men had flown over the Tangle with Survey instruments in the early days of Voor's first discovery. It registered life, but what kind of life no out-world built com or pick-up had ever been able to distinguish. From the air—I had seen the picture tapes—it looked like a thick, puffy, grey blanket—like smoke perhaps. Yet smoke would move, billow, thin or thicken and the Tangle did not.

From the ground it was an impenetrable mass of vegetation, so thick grown as to defy anything but a flamer to cut one's way in. Since there was plenty of empty land for which a settler did not have to fight, the Tangle was not so warred against. People had been lost in it, yes, flitters downed. If there had ever been any survivors of those crashes they had certainly never won free. As for getting out a guiding rescue call by com—that was impossible. A faculty the experts could not pin down made every com instrument go dead when one went so low as to skim just above the billows.

Yet now we were headed in a direction which could only eventually bring us to the Tangle's edge. As far as I knew there were not even any holding ruins in that direction and I could not understand what my father desired. When we nooned and ate our journey meat and drank from the wagon cans we had filled at the river, the brightness of the sun was dimmed by gathering clouds.

I saw Witol, our lead gar, a tough old bull on whose instincts any man might well depend (if he were Voor wise at all) lift his heavy head from grazing and turn west and a little south, his huge nostrils expanding as if to catch the slightest change in the wind which had risen with the gathering clouds. He snorted loudly and his team fellows also stopped their eating, likewise turning to face the west.

My father, who had been hunched silently moments earlier over a mug of res-tea which he had no more than sipped, got to his feet, and, like Witol, looked west into that wind. I did likewise, for the chill in the air grew sharper, and, though our senses are so much more the less than the beasts who accompanied us, I was at last able to catch a scent.

It was something which could not possibly come

from the open land before us. Only once had I picked up such an odor and that had been when my father's wanderings had led us well down the Halb into a place of swamps, unusual to find on the Big Land. There the same stench had struck us as that wet and slimy land had lain until the hot touch of midsummer sun. It was sickening—as if the wind now blew across some matter long gone into decay.

Illo moved a step or two out, away from the wagon, from the uneasy gars whose snorts had become grunts signaling rising uneasiness so that I went among them quickly, rubbing their big heads between the horns, making them aware of me. For gars seem, in spite of their awesome bulk, to depend upon our species when confronted by the strange and threatening. But the healer had her hands now raised to mask the lower part of her face, her eyes showing bright and intent above her interlaced fingers.

Though I strained to see, for our distance glasses were in my father's belt pouch and he had not taken them out, there was nothing but the rolling land and the wind blown grass. Illo turned her head a little and looked to my father.

"It—*they* move—"

His head jerked as if she had slapped him. In spite of the dark tint the sun had set upon him I saw a flush burn along his cheeks. He reached out and his hand fell upon her shoulder, tightened. He even shook her, until his control almost instantly returned and he moved away from her quickly, as if she herself were the source of some contagion and he wanted to put safe space between them.

"What do you know?" His tone was savage in its

harsh demand.

"I am from Voor's Grove." She had dropped her masking hands. There was no sign of outrage on her face, her calmness remained complete.

He might have forgotten all the rest. To him now she could be the only important thing in the world.

"What do you remember?" Some of the harshness had faded from his voice, but the demand remained, even more intense.

"Nothing— I was only three. I do not even know why I and Attcan, Mehil lived—though they were only cradle babies then. There was Krisan also. But surely you know of what happened at Voor's—you who are ever seeking to find the secret of the curse."

"You are a healer—you have talents—a gift—" it was as if he now pleaded with her.

She shook her head. "But no more memory than does your son. It is only this to know—some children, always Voor born, second generation, survive the Shadow curse. Do you not think that the medics, the off-worlds' 'experts' have not tried, poked and pryed, sent me into talk-sleep—done everything known to their science to wring an answer from me."

"They did that to you?"

Illo looked surprised. "Did they not also test your son in that same way?"

"No!" His denial was vehement. "No child should —why were they allowed to do this to you?"

She lost none of her serenity. "Because there was no one to speak for me and say they could not. Perhaps I should even be grateful to them, for it may have been their proving which released what you call my 'gift'. It is known that such a talent often manifests itself suddenly after illness or some injury. But what happened long in the past does not matter now—what does is the message this wind carries. Somewhere the Shadows must prowl."

Now he did take out the distance glasses, and, using them, turned his head slowly right to left and then back again even more slowly.

"Nothing—nothing which can be seen. There is no holding now in this way—"

"Not now," she agreed. "But bear you only a little more west and then north again and Voor's Grove will lie before you."

For the first time my father looked uneasy, as if she had caught him without any ready words.

"I am sorry, healer—" his voice was hardly above a mutter.

"There is no need for any distress. It is there I would go."

"Why?" I asked that from where I stood with my arm laid across Witol's wide back. The smell of his hide had driven out for me that wind borne stench of corruption.

It was a breech of custom, of good manners to ask such a question of a healer. Still I could not hold it back. In our wanderings we had visited near all of the foresaken holdings of the north, but never had my father returned to Mungo's, nor did I expect him to. What lay at the place of her past life which drew her now?

"Why?" she repeated. She did not look at me, or even at my father, rather into the distance, as if she needed no glasses but already could pick out there her destination. "Why? I do not know, but it is a call—one

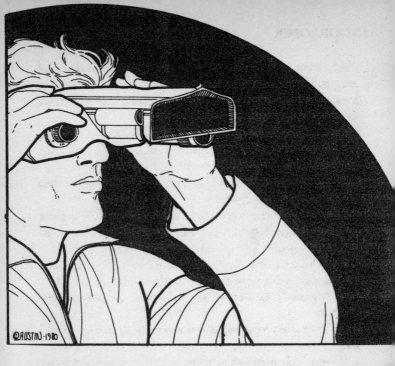

I cannot ignore."

"There can be no one there," my father pointed out. "It is not good to see what was once—"

He had hesitated but she finished the sentence for him calmly:

"A part of my life? I cannot remember. Perhaps if I returned there I could. What they did to me has left me with the need to know, only until now I did not feel that so strongly. Now it has become a call, like to such which the talent makes a part of us when there lies sickness and suffering somewhere and no help to hand. I cannot turn back—"

Though the clouds had grown heavier the wind had fallen away. I could no longer smell that stench. Loper that I was, and so weatherwise, I dared to speak up to my father:

"There is a storm coming—and we have no shelter."

Storms on the wide plains can be deadly—a strike of lightning out of the sky can kill man and beast. The torrent of autumn rain is always chill, and, more often than not, brings a burden of hail. I have seen such stones bury themselves half into the earth by the force of their fall, they being near large enough to cover most of my outstretched palm.

The gars were bellowing now, turning their backs to what wind there was. Witol threw up his head, sounded a summoning call. I leaped aside away from him, knowing that no voice or hand, no matter how accustomed he might be to it day by day, would hold him now. We were only lucky that we had out-spanned and that the half-maddened animals would not drag the wagon with them.

They went, their ropey tails up, their eyes rolling in growing terror. My father wasted no time in worry over whether we might round them up once again, or whether they would run on until exhausted, or per-haps come to earth with broken legs caught in some grass-hidden hole. Once more he caught Illo by the arm, to draw her swiftly to the wagon, pushing her up to me, where I had leaped to the foreseat, with as little ceremony as if she had been a bale of such goods as could take rough handling.

We near tumbled back into the living section with hardly time to scramble out of my father's way as he threw himself after. Then we were both up, he and I, making fast the flap covering, moving along the sides

of the wagon from one section to the next to test each cover latch and pushing the heaviest part of what we carried into the center as a makeshift anchor against the fury on its way.

The dark was now that of night. We did not light any lamp. Such, too, might become an added danger if what we expected came to pass. And it did.

That wind which had come early was but the gentlest of breezes against the force which slammed against the wagon, its roar enough to make anyone deaf. There had been a change in the direction of the fury; it blew from the west yet seemed to be altering towards the north. Under and around us our transport shuddered, shook, seemed to cower closer to the earth. If we had only had time we could have dug out beneath its wheels, letting it sink lower to the ground for anchorage. But that time had not been granted us.

The screech of the wind, which arose higher and higher in the scale like the scream of a woman under torture, was endless. I did not hesitate to crouch on my knees, my hands over my ears to shut out what I could of that fury. The wagon moved—swaying first from side to side until I was sure we could crash, then ahead, as if the wind had some intelligence and so had taken us prisoner.

I was thrown forward and landed against another form. Our arms reached out, caught at each other's bodies. I was locked with Illo in an embrace of stark fear when the hail struck with the same punishing force as the wind which bore it.

3.

The wagon continued to rock. Also it was again moving forward as if the wind was exerting full force against it. Though the grasslands might seem, under their covering of growth, to be flat surface, they were not. There were dips and hollows, small rises here and there, so that our transport now trembled on the edge of being completely thrown from its wheels and I could not understand how we continued to remain upright.

I had known autumn storms before, ridden out many of them. However the force of this blow exceeded anything in my memory. All one could feel was the helplessness of uncontrol, over even his own person. While always the sound of that blasting wind, the battering of hail over and around us, continued.

Were we being driven back towards the river as the gars had earlier fled? I could not be sure, but I believe that that was *not* so. The wind instead of battering us south was bearing us west and north—in the very direction we had been heading. Yet what could anyone make sure of in this chaos?

How long that thundering, howling storm possessed

us as prisoners I could not tell. The dark continued. In time I loosed my hold on Illo and strove to push aside those containers which, for all their travel lashing, had broken loose and thudded into our bodies with force enough to crack ribs or break bones, if they were to hit squarely.

My first efforts were blind, more the instinctive reaction of one who had always lived on the edge of peril and whose body reflexes took over even when his thoughts were awry. Then I began to gain hold of myself as it came as a clear stroke to cut through my own haze of fear that, though my father had entered the wagon in good time, he was not joining me in doing what could be done to secure the lashings.

I called him, and the roar, the thud of hail made so much sound I could not hear my own voice. Having done what I could to relieve us of immediate danger of being crushed, I crept on hands and knees through the thick dark to the fore of the wagon where I had seen him last come through the opening and turn to lash down the flap door.

The wagon was still rocking forward, and I held one arm out to fend off anything which might yet be adrift. With my other hand I groped ahead, striving to find— to touch him.

My fingers brushed trail leather, closed upon what could only be his upper arm. But he did not move at my touch, and there was a looseness— The wagon made another of its threatening side dips and his body slid, until I managed to reach and support it.

He lay with his head heavy against my shoulder now, my questing hand felt stickiness draining down his face, and it was plain he was unconscious. Light—

I must have light—!

Now the wagon itself was filled with the smell of spilled saloil. We used the lanterns of the trek people rather than the very costly unit rods from off world. There was no place outside Portcity or one of the mine compounds to recharge those. To try to spark a light with oil free-flowing might well add a final disaster to our situation.

I attempted to discover the extent of his hurts by touch alone, but I dared not examine him fully lest some unwary pressure of my hands might make his situation worse. Though I bent over him until our faces near touched I could not, in this uproar, hear his breathing, though my finger tips located the throat pulse and there was an answer there. Was it strong and steady as it should be? I doubted that. There was nothing to be done—nothing until the storm blew out or finished its play with us in some drastic fashion.

Illo—a healer! She would know—could give aid— Where was she?

The wagon lurched, tipped forward. I was jammed heavily against the fore part of the wagon, my father's inert weight lying half across me. The cargo! It had been well stowed. However, the lashings and bolted rods which held it were never meant to take this kind of punishment! I thought of two of the crates—they contained machines too heavy to transport by the miners' flitters and so consigned to our slower service. If those now broke loose they might even smash forward from the rear compartment to crush us. I struggled to free myself from under my father's body so that I might loose the door flap—make sure there was a small chance of escape.

Only there was no time. Whatever hollow lay before us now was deeper, more precipitous than any ordinary dip in the plains. The tilt of the wagon assumed a sharper angle. Then—the fore part hit.

We were stopped in the mad race which the wind had urged us into. Continued wind pressure now at the back might flip the whole transport entirely over. I held my breath waiting for that to happen.

Dimly I became aware that the pounding of the hail had ceased, and though the wind continued to batter us it lacked the last ultimate fraction of strength to send us end over end. I drew a deep breath, my whole body tense as I tried hard to listen. Had that continual roar dulled my hearing, or was it that the storm had spent the worse of its attack and was dying at last?

It was true that the wagon had stopped, slanted sharply towards the fore. As far as I could tell the cargo in the back was not battering down the two partitions between us. I shifted with care from under my father's weight, edging around his crumpled body to fumble with the lowest of the second flap lashings. Light—if we could only have a fraction of light!

The flap edge gave and I dragged it up. What came into the battered mess of what had been our home was a grey twilight, but steadily growing stronger.

My father lay beside me. There was a dark stream of blood down the side of his face spreading from the hair on the right side of his head. He was struggling to breathe, and now, with the dying of the storm fury, I could hear moans bubbling from his lips. Only there was red froth showing also at the corners of his mouth, spreading down his chin.

Illo crawled forward. She lifted a hand to signal that

I try to straighten him out, then edge back that she might see his hurts. Fortune had favored us in this much—we had her gift to depend upon now.

Her finger tips touched very lightly that matted patch of hair. Having seen healers at their task I knew that, though she knelt with closed eyes, having to steady herself against the angle of the flooring with her other hand, she was "seeing" after their strange fashion the extent and nature of his injury. Then her fingers slid down to his chest which I had quickly laid bare and once more she traced back and forth with the slightest of touches.

So much had the wind now died I was able to hear his labored breathing as well as those moans of pain. Now I heard the words I had so anxiously waited for:

"He is badly injured." She did not try to spare me and for that I was very glad. "There is a crack in his skull, and his ribs are broken. He must be aided, and quickly— My pack—"

She looked into the welter of stuff on the floor. I was busy with the rest of the lashing of the door flap. It was plain that broken bones could not be tended in this place. We would have to move him to where his body could lie straight and she would have the room to work upon him.

The flap open, I looked out. The day was now light —though there was no sign of sun. Immediately facing me was a hillside down which washed streams of water as thick as my wrist. When I thrust head and shoulders out to see more, it was plain that the wagon had come to rest, almost as a stopper might be pounded into a bottle, in one of those grass-hidden gullies which are to be found in the plains to carry off the water after just such storms.

That water which flowed down the walls was now rising about the fore of the wagon itself, fast enough to suggest that in a very short time it might wash high enough to lap into our present perch. We must get out and that quickly—but to try to carry an unconscious man through the rising flood was impossible. I made this report to Illo. She nodded, but did not raise her eyes from my father's face.

I crawled around them as best I could and up the slope formed by the other part of the wagon. The latch on the second compartment yielded easily enough. Beyond, though a few of the smaller containers had jammed themselves to this end (doubtless most of their fragile contents was now useless), I had no barrier against my drawing myself along by hand holds on those same shelves to the hatch of the end cargo section.

It all depended now on how well our restraints had worked there; I could open the hatch to find it barricaded by those machinery-filled crates which I could not shift by myself. Thumbing the lock-bar I discovered that just that had happened. There was a solid surface of crate facing me and no way from this side that I could hope to push it aside.

Back I went, fear riding on me, for I knew that for my father it could well be a matter of time, very little time. I stopped in the first cargo compartment only long enough to shoulder a coil of rope, though I had very little hope of being able to use that as it could be done only if there were two or three men to bring full strength to bear.

"No way out back there." Just as Illo had been

frank with me, so did I return the same truth in my report.

"We must hurry," was her only answer. That was one I had already guessed for myself.

I dropped down into the rising water, the wagon holding the major push of the current away from me. Now I could clearly see what had happened. We had blown into quite a deep crevice. There was thick brush on both banks and sight of that gave me my first fraction of dim hope. It would depend entirely on how far down those roots reached and with what tenacity they clung to the ground in which they were now buried. If the streams of descending water loosened the soil, what I planned was near impossible.

Though the brush resisted my climb, I had the wagon itself to pull against. The front wheels were nearly under the rising water now, but the back ones rested deeply up slope and I could drag myself through the whipping, briary stuff which laced my skin with a network of clawed scratches, until I reached the back of the wagon. There I loosened the latch and flung it wide open, to see that it was the largest and heaviest of the crates which jammed entrance at the other end of the section.

Now I tested the brush, paying no attention to the saw-edged leaves, the thorns which cut into my hands. My choice was one near the lip of the gully. There was no water running there within a good space on either side, and, in spite of all my sudden jerks and longer, deliberate pulls, it did not stir. I would have to chance dependence upon its support.

Back I crawled into the compartment, making fast one end of my rope with loper's knots which would

hold even a maddened gar. A gar! Never in my life have I wanted anything as much as Witol or one of the herd to stand waiting at that moment. But they were gone— I hoped they had reached some shelter before the full fury of that wind and hail had struck.

With the other end of the rope looped well about me I went again to my bush. Its inner trunk was thick, perhaps as large as my thigh, but I had to slash and cut with my belt knife to slice away the branches which were so close springing one could not reach that trunk without such clearage. Then the rope was around the trunk. I tested it the best I could, before I swung my whole weight upon it, throwing myself deliberately down slope. I brought up with a gasp of pain. Nor had that moved the crate barrier.

"Loose the end for me."

Gasping for breath I swung half way around, one hand on the up-tilted wheel to steady myself. Illo, her breeches plastered to her legs, her browned hands reaching out, had joined me before I knew it.

Two of us might do it. We could but try. Now she was only another pair of hands as far as I was concerned, an addition of strength. At my nod as I still fought to get back my breath, she took from where they were tucked into her girdle a pair of gloves and drew them on. As a healer, I guessed, she could not risk the sensitivity and skill of her fingers in the rasping punishment mine had taken. That done, she did not hold back any from twisting the rope with closed fists. Above her I settled myself for another effort.

"Now!"

The quick jerk, to be followed by a pull in which I knew we put both our strength. It moved! Loosed out of its tight jam against the door the crate appeared to give easily now, and I saw, as I turned my head, the edge of the obstacle visible in the wagon opening—then it tottered, fell forward into the brush, splintering and breaking the mass of greenery with its weight.

I threw the rope from me, was already up within the wagon bed, heading for the compartment door. Illo was on my heels as I pushed through the second section to reach our living quarters. There I found she had already accomplished what I would have believed impossible for her strength, for my father was a big man, spare of flesh perhaps, but heavy of bone. He had been straightened out upon a length of board she had loosened from the side of a bunk, for those could be dismantled at need for extra space. His body arranged as best she might, it was only necessary now for me to once more use the rope, setting one end of it with her hold, to bind my father's blanketed body to that board.

Half carrying, half dragging him so we retraced our way just as the first waters of the rising stream licked across the forepart of the wagon. It might be injurious to move him, but now that was the lesser of evils. Lowered from the wagon end and still immobilized on the board, we transported him on through the brush to the lip of the gully, though twice we had to lay down our burden so I could knife-hack a passage for us.

When we reached the torn earth of the edge over which the wagon had plunged I was so beat by weariness that I had only strength enough to see our burden over and lying face up in the matted, water-soaked grass under the clearing sky. I longed to throw myself down beside him, but there was that which must be saved from the wagon lest the water sweep away what might come to be our future means of life.

Three times I made the journey down and up, each time spurring myself to the descent and climb. Up there now was Illo's precious pack which she had already opened as she worked over my father, food, damp blankets, our stunners and tanglers, two night torches, a com which might or might not work after the way it had been bounced about during our wild journey, and anything else I chanced upon which would serve us.

It was plain that without the gars there was no hope of pulling free the wagon. At least none that I could see. There was always the chance that the com might have range enough to reach Dengaugha—of that I could not be sure. The miners had a flitter, and, though I had little idea now of where we were in connection with their settlement, on this plain there should be some way of raising a signal for help which would guide air borne rescue to us.

The heavy pelt of the rain was luckily over, but it had left the grass in which we made now an uncomfortable camp site soaked and flattened by the burden of water which had fallen. I had the emergency heat unit from the wagon, though its active life was so limited we could not hope for it to last long.

Illo asked my aid in strapping my father's ribs with bands cut from one of the blankets. She had also bandaged his head. Now, wrapped in near all the coverings I had managed to pull free from the water rising so steadily in the fore part of the wagon, he lay beside that single unsteady flame. His face was grey rather than pale beneath the weathered brown, and I could not bear to look at him often. At each time I did a fear I would not allow myself yet to face arose in me like some choking illness.

I set up a lean-to of planks torn from the inner fittings of the wagon, thatched as well as I could manage with the brush I slashed free. The clouds had scudded south to allow a watery emergence of the sun. I climbed to the highest of the small rolling hills which lay beneath the blanket of grass and turned the distance glasses on the land around, hoping against hope to pick up sight of the gars.

There was nothing, save a bird or two wheeling and dipping back and forth across the sky. We were left with only the chance that the com might summon aid, and I trudged back to the lean-to and got it out.

Such off-world artifacts were always prized and kept in the best repair possible. These were too costly when shipped by Spacers for the average Voorsman to own. Though I knew how to repair one, there were certain materials which could not be substituted by anything known on Voor. The men of the holdings worked well with their hands—in wood and stone. There was some primitive and experimental work done with metal—the forging of large tools and the like. But small precision objects which were the result of centuries of technological know-how could not be duplicated.

It was with the greatest of suspense that I opened the com carrying case to inspect how its contents had fared. The round of metal, with the mike disc lying upon it, had been packed as best we knew, so I had to pull out wads of grass-cotton to free the disc and dial. I could see no breakage as I worked the thing carefully

out of its soft nest. Then I pried loose the back of the inner case. Wires, works, I traced what I could see without taking the unit apart. My spirits arose a little as I could detect no fracture. Now it depended upon the range.

Where the wind had driven us I could not tell, though when I had used the distance glasses I had been sure that the ominous smudge which marked the Tangle was far more visible. Perhaps we had been blown on to cover more distance than we could have covered in several days at the usual trek pace.

Illo had been tending a small pan to which she had fitted a long handle so she could hold it well over the flame of our heat without scorching her fingers. She seemed entirely intent upon her task and did not even look up as I readied the com and raised the mike, repeating into it the call letters which had been assigned us in Portcity and which must be on record at Dengungha. Three times I uttered those and waited for a reply. What came back to me was a crackle so loud and disturbing that I had to lay the mike down upon the box; that outburst of sound was enough to hurt ears already assaulted by the storm's long roar.

Patiently I went through the same procedure twice more, with no better result. If there was not any fault in the com, then there must be some freakish effect left by the storm itself which interfered with reception. Regretfully I had to fit the com back into its case.

Illo appeared satisfied with the bubbling contents of her pan for she set that aside until she hunted out a bag of small grass-cotton puffs. Wetting one of those in the pan's contents, she sponged my father's lips, gently forcing his mouth open so she could squeeze her improvised sponge and so get some of the liquid into him.

He no longer moaned. The very inert limpness of his body frightened me, though I determined not to let her know that. What liquid she had managed to get into his mouth was dribbling out again at one corner. Now she did look up at me.

"When I do thus," once more she held the sponge ball above his mouth, "you rub his throat—gently—downward. We must get him to swallow some of this. It is strengthening, a barrier against the shock and chill which follows bad wounds."

I followed her orders. My father's flesh was indeed cold under my touch. Resolutely we worked, I under her orders, until he did swallow and she was able, by patient concentration, to get perhaps a third of the contents of the small pan into him.

"We shall let him rest now." Her own hand rested for a long, measuring moment on his forehead below the bandage.

"He—how is he?" For the first time I asked, dreading even as I did what she might answer.

Slowly she shook her head. "These are bad hurts. I think that one of the broken ribs may have entered into a lung. As for the crack in the skull—we know so little of what may happen after such as that. However, he lives, and, as long as he holds to life, then we can also hold to hope. I wish we could get him to some cover better than this—"

I got up, frustration and anger at what had happened building up in me, so I must keep a sharp rein on my tongue and swallow the words I wanted to say. It was none of her doing, or his, or mine, that this thing had happened. Still something in me wanted to make me lash out and scream with rage that it was this way. Once more I left our sorry camp and tramped back to my small hillock which certainly raised me very little above the rest of the plain.

In the gully the water washed high now, hiding the fore of the wagon, which shook now and then as the current tried to break or bear away this barrier against its even flow. I turned my glasses along the path of the gully itself. It was truly a flow from the north. Perhaps it even traced its beginning back to the mountains beyond the Tangle where Survey ships had flown to map from the sky, but, to my knowledge, no one of my race had ever gone. They were stark, those mountains, sharp, jagged peaks, showing like teeth between the gaping jaws of some monster. Dire, and dark, and not for humankind.

There was, as I watched the flow of water in the gully, storm wrack coming with it now. Brush such as grew along the banks, uprooted when the waters gnawed the soil from about their roots, bounced and wavered along. Some of the stuff came to rest uneasily against the wagon, building up more tightly the damming barrier that had begun.

Now there was other movement in the water. My hand flew to stunner butt and I had that out of my holster when I saw, and knew it was no vision, an ugly, armored head rise above the surface, round, unblinking, but dead white eyes, regard the brush and the wagon.

This was certainly like no creature I had seen before, not of the grass plains. I took a running leap from the hill, was down at the gully's rim as a webbed and taloned paw, larger than my own hand, slopped up from the water, drew arching claws down the wagon's body, seeking some hold.

That it found. A second paw now wavered aloft hunting similar anchorage. I pushed right to the edge of the drop, my weapon ready. The thing had already opened jaws wide enough to near split its head in two and those were tooth ringed—I could be well sure it was a flesh eater.

The monster did not move clumsily in spite of the bulk of its body, for beneath the longish neck the rest of it was wide, out of proportion with the head, while the legs appeared much too slender to support it. This thing, I thought, must spend much time in the water. Now it hauled itself to the top of the wagon, and, lifting higher that ugly head, gave voice to an ear-rasping grunting.

"What is it?" Illo came up beside me.

"I don't know. But—"

The head shot around, made a dart in our direction. The eyes looked blind, white balls only, without even the faintest slit to suggest a pupil. Yet it was evident that the thing saw us, judged us either enemy or prey. Still grunting it drew itself wholly out of the water, showing other hook-clawed legs, and started to climb along the upward slant of the wagon.

I centered the stunner on its head, set the charge on full, and fired. I might as well have flipped a twig for it did not even shake its head as if momentarily dizzy. Yet a gar, a sand cat, a jaz would have been plunged into instant unconsciousness.

The clawed forefeet were already raking into the brush from which I had hacked our escape path. Perhaps on land we could hope to outrun it, or dodge, but not with the unconscious man lying beside the fire. I might have fired too soon, my aim a fraction off—

This time I made myself concentrate only on that weaving ugly head. There was a point directly between the white eyes—I settled on that for my target. Then Illo's voice broke through my strained concentration.

"Aim for the neck, where it joins the back!"

What did she know about it? She by her own words had never seen this thing before.

"Aim there!" her voice had the crack of an order. "Its brain—I cannot sense a brain at all!"

Her words did not mean much. But a straightforward shot had not brought it down. I had once seen a gar paralyzed when a stunner merely clipped its backbone. Could that trick work here?

Though every instinct told me that I might be wrong, I changed, in that last instant, the angle of my ray shot. I did aim where that weaving neck sank into the foul, scaled and flabby bag of body.

Full strength, and I held it past the first shot, refusing to let myself remember I could so exhaust the whole charge completely.

The neck snapped straight up into the air as if, instead of a ray, I had laid across it the leash of a whip to torment the flesh. Then it looped forward, falling limply, so that the head dragged along the brush as the body itself, the taloned paws relaxing their hold, slid down and down, slipping at last from the wagon into the stream, where it sank beneath water now brown with silt.

©AUSTIN-1980

4.

There was a brief swirl of water against the pull of the current and then nothing at all. If the thing was indeed a water dweller it could lie hidden there, so covered now was the surface with floating debris of the flood and a film of mud, only to emerge once again to attack. We must move away. But to do that—

When I spoke my fear aloud Illo nodded. "This thing—I have never even heard of its like before," she said slowly as she stood still gazing at the flow of water as if she expected any moment to see that hideous head rise again. "At least in the south. It might be a dweller in those swamp lands perhaps—but where—"

I was facing north-west. During my travels as loper I had seen many strange creatures. In fact it had been one of my father's concerns to record any new living thing, were it flyer, crawler, or growing plant, which we came across. So detailed had been this work of his that it had first led me to wonder if he had not, in that unknown past which he never shared with me, been connected with Survey.

Not that he shared officially any of his knowledge

with the authorities at Portcity as far as I knew. It was as if he was driven by some need of his own to learn all which it was possible to gather about Voor. However, like Illo, we had never heard of nor seen anything like the monster of the flood.

As for a swamp—there were some in the south, yes. Still none so large a spread of country to give living space to this size creature. While to the north—

I had raised my head now, gazed beyond the swiftly flowing, ever rising waters which were now rocking the wagon even more dangerously, so that it canted to the right and might well be shortly engulfed. The stream, though born of the fury of the storm, lay in a bed which water had already carved, and it came from the north-west—that same direction in which the Tangle made its stain across the healthy plains.

Was that mass of entwined vegetation a cover for a swamp? It could well be, though so thick a growth seldom was a part of any swampland I knew. And the beast we had fought off was of a size unsuited to the density of that maze men had not been able to force any path through as long as planet record existed.

Yet so sinister was the reputation of that massed growth I could well accept that it might give living room to any number of monsters. Not that that had any meaning for us now. We must concentrate on getting ourselves and my father to some civilized shelter. If we could not raise the mines with the com, then we must somehow trek south, back to the holding where we had been only days earlier.

I set about once more securing from the wagon such materials which might be of use. Spare of frame as my father was, we could not carry him between us and achieve any great distance, except at less than a usual walking pace. I believed that we had no time for that. Still there were other ways which we could attempt, and I salvaged gear, venturing gingerly time and again into the rocking, tilting wagon.

Water already washed into the front compartment and the wagon was near on its side as the stream gnawed steadily at the bank in which the back wheels were embedded. I had given Illo the second stunner and she had stationed herself to watch for any more water-dwellers.

The clouds had finally all gone and the sun made a dim showing, but it was already far down the horizon. I had so little time. Also I was so tired that my hands shook as I strove to unfasten lashings, bundle up all I could, perhaps bringing a lot which I had no need for in my desire not to miss anything which would be of value.

There was no lifting out the cargo. That, unless we could contact the mines and gain aid there, must be written off as a total loss. But the small stuff I bundled out hit and miss, passing up the awkward armloads I gathered to the girl who piled them about her sentry post.

I worked until the wagon gave a warning lurch so that I leaped clear just as it went over on its side while water boiled up and in. Somehow I won back up the slope and fell, gasping for breath with a band of permasteel seemingly fastened about my middle, drawing always inward as might the jaws of a slowly closing trap.

Illo had already carried some of the goods back to our improvised camp. Much I knew I could not deal with now. It was all I could do to stagger towards that flare which had now become a beacon, there to collapse again, my body one ache from head to foot.

I remember drinking from a pan Illo handed me, thinking dimly that we must set a guard for the night. Most of the grass plains had few predators, and all of those, as lopers knew, were not only night hunters but afraid of fire. However, there was still the water—and what could come out of it. Only I could not make any effort to so much as reach for the stunner which was thrust into my belt, even keep my eyes open. Instead fatigue settled on me in a smothering blanket, drew me in and covered me, as might the Tangle itself.

I awoke— The stars were brilliant overhead; the orange-red of Voor's moon was a ball hanging near directly over me. It was one of those instant awakenings which come to those who live always on the edge of the unknown, whose instincts and inner warning systems have become trained to signal alerts as potent as any a starship might possess.

There was the light on the ground— Three of our salvaged camp lamps had been filled, trimmed, and set out, burning sturdily. Beyond them lay an unsorted mound of all I had pulled from the wagon. After I had given out, the girl must have brought much of it here. The girl—!

She sat hunkered down beside the plank which served my father as a bed. The lamps gave her face a deceptive ruddiness. Her eyes were closed, but the hand lying beside her held grip on the other stunner.

I was ashamed at my own failure. At that moment my pride was cruelly hurt that I, who was supposed to be the toughened loper, had failed what was surely a good part of my duty. She had even pulled over me one of the gar fleece blankets. That I now hurled aside in my flare of temper at my own collapse.

Yet that temper only raged for an instant. Something had awakened me; my plains knowledge assumed control. I could hear the water in the gully, though that did not sound to me as if it were now made by any rushing stream. Perhaps that storm born flood was subsiding.

My loper's belt was about me, slung with those tools and aids any treker must depend upon. Beside the stunner holster, the weight of my knife was against my hip as I stood up. My hand rested steadily about its hilt as I slowly turned my head from east to west, and then faced around to look north.

There was the night wind, yes, but it did not sing tonight through the long grass which had been so beaten down by the storm. Nor did it carry with it that strange odor which had been a part of it before the coming of the storm. If some scavenger prowled beyond the reach of our fire, the visitor made no sound.

For a moment or two I had a sudden leap of hope—the gars! Had Witol managed to find his way back, perhaps heading as herd leader the others of the team? I whistled softly that call which the massive beast always answered if he was within range of hearing.

There was no snorting, no sound of those hooves thudding on the plains ground. Yet there was something—a sound, a feeling had brought me out of sleep and now held me tense and listening. If my father—I knew that my hard-learned knowledge of the loper's world was nearly only the beginning of a child's first reading tape compared to his. I had seen him so alerted many times in the past, and always there had been excellent reason.

Sight was not going to serve me beyond the lantern glow; smell and sound had brought me nothing—yet. I crossed to where Illo huddled, stooped and drew the stunner from her lax grasp. With that at ready, saving my own for an emergency, I began a slow circuit of our improvised camp, stopping every few paces, to listen, to stare out into the country with its moon-painted patches of light and dark.

Nothing to be detected. The grass was so heavy with water that it was beaten towards the ground. Anything trying to reach us through that would have made both sound and movement which I could easily pick up. There remained the stream. I unhooked my night torch from my belt. Its charges must be carefully conserved as there was only one small box of them which I had managed to drag away from the flood. Still I thumbed the control button on high and aimed the wide beam of frosty light down into the gully.

The weight of the wagon, its forepart pushed by the stream, had broken one of the embedded rear wheels, so now it lay on its side. Were my father whole and the gars to hand, its repair and return to the trek would have been a hard job but not an impossible one. Under the present circumstances I could not hope to draw the vehicle out again.

That river which had been such a force had greatly subsided. Though its surface was still opaque with silt and muddy swirls, the current had lessened and was no longer high enough to give cover to any such beast as had threatened us.

Though the dropping of the water would certainly have partly uncovered the bulk of the creature's body were it still inert from the ray, there was no serrated, scaled back showing. The thing had either been borne well down stream, or had swum away of its own accord. To my most searching survey nothing lay there but the wreck of the wagon and the steadily lessening flow of water.

I had made a circle about our camp without result. Yet—I knew. There was something which had awakened me, something out there somewhere—waiting—

I thought of what my mother's kinswoman had said —Shadow touched. Oh, I had heard the expression before but then it had not meant—me. What had happened when the death had come to the northern holdings? Why had a child here, some infants there—all second generation—escaped whatever doom it was which had blasted whole settlements out of existence? Why should we not remember?

Once more I reached back in my own mind— No, there was only riding the gar under the sun, my father tramping beside the beast. I could not even clearly remember *him;* the gar was far more vivid in my mental picture.

Was that because riding was strange and wonderful, an exciting thing for a small boy? The settlements and holdings used gars, yes—but those were lesser in size, in strength, in all that which might impress a small child, than the animals a loper trained and lived with most of his life.

I thought of my father's constant interest in the deserted and ruined sites where the Shadows had

struck—risking his life to explore such. Why did men speak of "Shadows"? If there were no survivors who could report on the nature of the danger—then who had given them that name?

Again I searched memory and could find nothing to answer my own question. I had heard of "Shadows" as a danger, as doom and death, all my life—still, in spite of all my father's searching I had never been told why that unknown menace in the north had been so named. It was as if there was some inward flinching away in me which kept me from such speculation, a barrier—

As I slipped once more around our camp I not only searched the night-covered land for the reason for my waking, my uneasiness, but another part of my mind was busy—for the first time I could honestly remember—in asking those questions. Three times I went around just within the farthest gleam of the lanterns.

Instead of being able to reassure myself that nothing waited in the water-drenched, moonlit land, my feeling that we were under observation of some sort grew deeper. I found myself hunching my shoulders against my will, as if I expected a knife to come whistling through the air to strike into my flesh, a blaster to crisp me, skin and bone. I waited for a long space each time I stood at the edge of the gully, my torch beam striking down at the water which was reduced so rapidly now in its flow it was as if the ground itself was a sponge soaking up that fluid in huge quantities.

At last I turned aside from my self-appointed sentry's beat and went directly to where my father lay, covered with one of the blankets. In the light which was less glaring than my torch, his face was drawn, the bones seeming to stand out beneath the skin as if in these short hours some deadly illness had eaten through his resistance. And—

His eyes were wide open. Not only open but aware. They met mine with intelligence, a compulsion which brought me to my knees beside him. I might have at that moment been no older than the small boy in my memory of the past.

Illo had washed the blood from his face, bandaged his wounds. The blanket was pulled up to his throat, masking the broken body. Pain must have made those lines so deep there now, but he had forced it away from him, under his control. I read that, and I do not know how I did it.

I saw his lips move with effort. There was a beading of sweat across what forehead the bandage did not cover. Driven by what lay in his eyes I leaned very low above him so my ear was close to those struggling lips.

"North—to Mungo—" his words were a mere wisp of sound. "North—I—I—must—lie—in Mungo. Swear this, swear it!" Somehow he had gathered the strength to make those last four words ring out, above the tortured whisper, clear and strong as he might have given the signal for the gars to be on the move.

There was a bubble of red again showing at a corner of his mouth. He coughed thickly, rackingly. The bubble burst, and blood spewed forth. But his eyes never loosed their hold on mine. His lips worked again—but there was only that terrible, tearing cough which brought out gouts of blood instead of the words.

"I swear—!" There was no other answer which could ease him in this time; that I understood.

The bright glint in his eyes still held strong and clear for a long moment after we made that pact. I reached beneath the edge of the blanket, found his hand and held it. In him there yet remained some strength, for his fingers tightened in my hold, gripping mine with a force I would not have believed he was still able to summon.

He did not try to speak again. But he kept his eyes open and on mine and we held that grasp. Was it for long? There was no measurement of time. I am not sure when it was that his head moved a fraction on the folded blanket we had used to pillow it, when he looked beyond me at something else. For that he did see something in that last moment I shall always swear. What it was remained his secret, but I think in some manner it was a comfort, for the pain lines lessened, and there was a new peace—an expression I realized I had never seen on my father's calm face before. He was in that moment younger, eager, a man I did not know, that it had never been for me to know.

I still sat by him as the moon dropped low in the night sky, but what I guarded now was nothing—an outworn coat, a forgotten and unneeded garment. My father was gone and left in me an emptiness which grew deeper and wider, making a space into which I thought I might even fall and never climb out of again. I had had no life which had not held him always there —what could I do now?

I started. The touch on my shoulder then was as if a blaster had seared across unshielded flesh.

"He has taken his own way, that lay in his mind from the beginning."

I looked up at the girl, my anger hot enough to burn

away the uncertainty of moments earlier.

"He had strength—he would not have—done what you say!" I denied her words fiercely. For I had seen once or twice in my roving life those who died of what seemed minor illnesses or superficial hurts because they had no wish to live. My father was not to be numbered among them. I think at that moment my rage boiled up in me, fed by the hurt of my own loss, might have led me to strike out physically at her.

"He was tired—very tired, and he was one of those who know—"

She did not draw away from me. Her face and voice still held the calm of her calling. That serenity began to react on me as it always did when one came in contact with the healers.

"One who knows what?" I demanded.

"It is given to some of us to understand and know when the great change draws near. He was a man who has been driven many years by that which he could not accept—he had already begun to believe that he must reach beyond our life to understand."

Her words dropped into my mind one by one as one might cast pebbles into a pool and watch the ripples spread outward to the edge of the surface and then break and go. That my father was a driven man—yes, that I had always known since I had grown into the age when one's world does not center only upon one's self as it does for a child. That he was ridden ever by the puzzle which remained beyond his solving, yes, that, too, was true. But that he would surrender— No! I bit back the harsh outburst which I might have used to greet that. What remained to think on now—at this present—was not that he had died—doubtless of such hurts not even off-world medical wonders could heal—but that he had asked a promise of me and I was sworn to fulfill it.

How was that task to be accomplished? I did not even know for sure in what direction Mungo's lay or how far away. But that I would do this—that I must.

"I have sworn to him that he will lie in Mungo's—or what is still left of it," I told her. Somehow I shook my mind free of the frozen grip upon it, began to think of ways and means. Days of travel might lie ahead. I had no transport—even if I could raise the mine or the port on the com, I knew that I could get no one who would be willing to help.

Very well, alone I would do what I must. So I set to work. But when she saw what I brought out of the jumble of supplies Illo came forward, and, without a word, set about helping me. My father's body we sealed into the protect suit he had used all these years for exploring the Shadow-blasted ruins. There was a keg of plastaseal in the broken wagon, part of the shipment for the mine, used to repair their shelters there. Now it proved the outward seal, the encoffining for the body, until even the white suit was completely hidden by a swiftly stiffening green casing which under the sun became dura-hard.

Just as I had half thought out the transport for him alive, so did I now follow the same idea for him dead. The planks from the bunks I also sealed together with what was left of the plasta—forming a platform on which the enclosed body could be safely lashed.

I worked away most of the day, dealing with what supplies and tools I might use or improvise. Nor was I aware, as I worked, of anything but the job at hand,

driving myself to its doing. Only when I had fastened
the last rope and smeared the remaining drops of
plasta over those knots, did I stagger to the side of the
fire and take in shaking hands the bowl of food Illo
held out to me. I was halfway through gulping its contents when I heard the sound which brought me to my
feet, the food dribbling to the ground as the bowl
turned over in my grasp. Faint and far away, yes—! I
had no doubts that that was what I had heard.

Now I dropped the bowl entirely, put fingers to my
lips to aid in a distance piercing whistle. Gars—that
could have been the bellow of some wild herd bull, for
there were such, drifters from the ruined holdings.
Only, once a team was well united, it was the nature
of the great beasts to keep with their masters in a
strong relationship, and our gars had been unusually
united, even for their breed.

That they could have traced us over the wildness
where the stream had driven the wagon, that, too, was
not unknown. I had heard tales of gars who had traveled from one holding to another seeking the breeder
with whom they had been identified in training as
calves. That was why few of them could ever be sold
away from their trainers.

It was close to sunset, but there was light across the
land. I fumbled for my distance glasses after I had
whistled for the second time. Now I could pick up
greyish specks in the distance—three of them. Where
the others were—remembering the fury of the storm,
the beating of the hail, perhaps I could expect no more
than those.

Illo moved in beside me. "Yours?"

"I will wager it. But there are only three—"

"Not enough to raise the wagon," she commented.

I shook my head, my attention all for those distant dots which were growing larger by the moment. They were moving fast, at a trot, their horned heads now and then dipping groundwards as if they scented some trail. But there was no mistaking that larger bulk in the lead now—Witol! One who followed was his mate —Dru—and the third—he was a youngster whom we had put to the yoke only this season, a calf sired by Witol—Wodru.

With the gars I could well carry out my plan. Only, as I turned back to the fire confident that they would soon be shouldering their way to our camp, I remembered for the first time Illo and her own quest. I was bound to the task my father had set for me, but as trekmaster he had given her passage with us. The cargo we carried for the mine would be no problem— I could use the com as a set signal for the men there and give in that fashion a pick-up point so that they could find what might be salvaged. Illo's transportation was another matter. I must now take on the responsibility of seeing her safely to her own destination.

"Will you go on?" I asked bluntly. "Have you any map or guide?"

She looked up at me over her shoulder, for she had gone back to kneel by the fire and add to it some of the brush culled from beneath the growth where the rain had not left it sodden.

"Trekmaster's bond?" she held out her hands to the small flames. "No, I do not hold you to it, Bart s'Lorn. Such can be dissolved by mutual consent."

"I do not consent," I told her sharply. "With the gars we can pack enough supplies surely to see you to where you would go—"

"Very well then. Suppose I say now that I go to Mungo's—"

"Why?" I challenged her. "Because you know that I must journey there? But that is folly. I can see you to whatever holding—"

"Holding?" she interrupted me. "There is no holding or settlement—save that of the off-worlders—this far north—now."

"But you said—you had call, that you were needed. The off-worlders—?"

Her lips curved in a faint smile. "Would they drink my portions, allow my hands to draw any illness from them? They have no belief in such. Yes, I was called— but not by any messenger such as can be seen or heard. I told you—I am Shadow touched. As your father there is a need in me to know—to discover what I cannot remember. So— Mungo's fell to the Shadow doom as did Voor's Grove. Therefore, perhaps I can learn the nature of what I wish there as well as in the place from which I came."

I did not like it. Still it cannot be that any man says 'no' to a healer who declares that she has a call for aid. That she could not help my father was no reflection on her skill—for there are hurts past any healing. It was true that if I did not have to linger on my own journey to see her to her destination it would be the better. Still I was not satisfied within myself, though I could raise no adequate argument against such a journey.

The gars reached our camp and then I saw a thing which I had witnessed but once before in my life, for the three beasts, led by Witol went to the crude sled on which my father's body lay in the coffining I had devised and there stood for a space, Witol at the head, Dru on his right, Wodru on the left. The great team leader raised his three horned head and gave a cry which was not his usual deep-throated bellow, rather a keening which I have heard from those of his species when one of their own herd or team lay dead.

Three times did the gar sound his cry and then he turned, the other two falling in behind him, and they walked slowly and purposefully to me, Witol lowering his head now so that I could lay my flattened palm on the smooth hide between his great eyes as was also customary when one of his kind chose to serve a man of his own free will.

For near ten years of my life I had known Witol, yet never had he given me this salute. We had often speculated, my father and I, as to the intelligence of the gars—now I believed I had proof that they were indeed more than just the bearers of burdens which off-worlders classed them as being. Now I spoke to Witol and the others, greeting them by name as gravely and with as much courtesy as if they had been the people of some holding, thanking them for the offering of their service.

Thus we slept that night within the light of the lanterns, but more secure, for the gars could and did keep patrol. I thought earlier that I might never sleep well again, that memory would come to plague me with the knowledge of all I had lost. Only that was not so—perhaps the fatigue of my body won the battle with my mind, for I sank into a darkness which even dreams did not trouble.

5.

Among the gear which I had salvaged from the wagon were two things which I made use of in the morning. Though I was left with no way of transporting the heavy crates which had been ordered by the offworlders, still I, now by force of circumstances made trekmaster, must take what precautions that I could concerning the consigned cargo. So I set on the top of that small hillock beyond the lip of the gully a detect taken from the miner's own order. Sooner or later they would be in search, and that sound broadcast into the sky would register on the instruments of their flyers though it would not summon any other wanderers.

With the detect I left a tape recording of what had happened to us so that my father, even in death, would be cleared of unfair dealing or refusal to carry out a contract. Since loper's pride demanded this by their small but rigid code, I made sure this was done to the best of my ability.

We worked through the morning dividing all I had brought from the wagon, choosing that which was the most useful for what might lie ahead. I set aside tools, such off-world gadgets, which, if they failed in the wilderness of the plains, would be only useless burdens. For example, we needed no coms, for there would be no one in the north land to pick up any cry for help. So what we took were the necessities to which a loper could pare his packing when it was necessary.

There were the trail rations—the hard cakes of pressed and dried meats and grains produced nourishing food. I made another raid upon the wagon, detached two of the water carriers which were slung on the upward side I was still able to reach. Illo strained the rapidly dwindling water of the gully through a length of cloth and filled both of these as well as the supply would let her. Together they made a single load, one slung on either side of her back, for Dru.

Blankets folded into packs held extra charges for the stunners, our two tanglers, some simple tools, such as the hatchet which I had used to clear the brush in the gully, a coil of the rope which was so thin and could be looped into small lengths and yet remain so tough even my belt knife had difficulty in slicing it through. We decided against the lanterns, taking instead all units for the two torches: that my father had worn on his belt and my own. Illo shouldered her own compact pack, and I had another like it put together with all I could think of which might be of use in the field. There was a second sling of packs for Wodru, and Witol bent to the harness I had cobbled together for the sled which held my father.

We ate a hasty meal when the sun was noon high and then started onward. One thing I had taken with me which might be considered as unnecessary burden were those tapes my father had dictated after each exploration of one of the deserted holdings, together with the reader. They had no like, I was sure, anywhere on Voor and if we could learn anything more of what lay before us, it might come only from those.

Across the gully we went. Nor did I look back at the wreck of the wagon. It was as if that part of my life was now finished, complete, and there was no need to think of any loss—save the greatest one of all and that we carried with us.

Our goal was that distant shadow of the Tangle, the ugly blot of which stretched across the far horizon. I had a map of my father's make, which I carried in my belt pocket, and I knew each marking on that as well as I knew the lines appearing on the palm of my own hand. For I had been with him when most of them had been set down. I had shown this chart to Illo before we broke camp and she had pointed to the northwest where there was only vacancy.

"Voor's Grove lies so—" she spoke with such conviction I did not doubt her. "Where is Mungo's?"

To my knowledge my father had never returned to that lost town once he had taken me out of it. Still he had marked it and in a separate way with a small sign like the blade of a drawn knife done in red. To my plains-wise observation it lay a little to the east from where we had crossed the gully. Nor would it be as close to the Tangle as Voor's Grove.

On this wide land there were few marks one could sight on as guides. The Tangle was the most obvious one, being the end of any march or penetration in this direction. So that we need only head on towards that and then prospect a little from our main trail to strike Mungo's. Or so I hoped—and made myself believe.

The gars moved onward at a steady pace which was not difficult for either of us to match. I had made no provision to lead any of the animals as a loper sometimes sets guide rope to the fore yoke of a wagon. Somehow I accepted that Witol understood what we chose to do and would himself willingly follow the same path.

The grass was lifting upright once more under the pull of the sun as the heaviness of the rain damp was loosed. As it brushed against us and the hides of the gars, we were soon wet to our knees, with patches of damp well up the animals' legs.

By mid-afternoon we came to a wallow-cupping and this brimmed full with the bounty left by the storm. The three gars drank their fill from one side of that already dropping level of water, while we did the same from the other. Nor were we alone. There was a scuttling in that grass, a fleeing of small things we could not see. In the muddy rim about the wallow was such a tracery of tracks it looked as if this had been a point of meeting for both birds and animals. I picked up those of species I knew, inspecting the mud patch carefully all the way around for any prints which might be left by the few predators hunting in the grass lands. Luckily I saw no claw prints of the scrowers—those sharp-beaked screaming furies who could outrace a running man and were ready to feed on anything smaller or weaker than themselves.

However it was only wise to put as much distance as possible between us and that pool before the coming of night. For that which would drink by day was in the main harmless. The true hunters emerged after dark. Witol might have been able to read my mind, for, once his thirst and that of his companions was quenched, he quickened pace to a trot and I broke into the loper's run to keep abreast of him. Twice I glanced at Illo, but she seemed able to keep up well with the other two gars and I was fast losing any fear that she would be a drag upon me. She could have well been trained by the same schooling as I had known for so many years.

There was no shelter on the plains. One felt naked, I discovered, without the wagon which had always served as the center part of any camp I had known. Still we must select a site before the coming of dark, having no lanterns to give us that small protection our own species find from fire or light as dusk closes in.

At length I settled on place backed by a ridge, one of those small conformations which the height of the grass half hid. That grass itself I hacked away to bare a stretch of ground. The sun had dried it sufficiently that it might be heaped into small mounds on which we could spread our blankets. Only I would set no fire to be a signal in the night.

The gars, loosed of their packs, grazed in a circle, now and then lifting a head with nostrils expanded to catch the rising night wind which carried no sickly taint in warning. We sat side by side, munching each on a single pressed cake of the journey food, discovering that every bite must be chewed a long time before it was soft enough to swallow.

During all the journey we had exchanged very few words. Now I wanted desperately to forget—if only for a short space—the mission which sent us north. Perhaps I should bring out the tapes and their reader, listen to my father's words in preparation for what might face us tomorrow, or the day after, or the day after that. For I could not calculate as to how long it would be before we would chance on what was left of Mungo's. Only, in that hour, I dared not do that. To listen so might break through the metal-hard resolve which kept me going. So, in a kind of desperation, I asked a question:

"You travel like a loper—have you gone far?"

She retorted with another question:

"This north land is not strange to you, is it?"

"No, if you have heard of my father you must also know what men say—said—of him. That he hunts what he cannot find and pushes into places better left alone."

"I know. That is why I sought him—and you—out. You ask if I have traveled far—yes—both in body and in mind—"

"I do not understand—" If one traveled in body, then certainly one's mind also went the same distance, I thought foggily. I was becoming aware now of my fatigue. Perhaps I still could not think clearly as I had before the storm had struck and changed my life.

"What do you know of healers?" She sat crosslegged on her blanket-spread sleeping mound. The sun was down but we still had twilight so I could see her face. That was smooth of expression; now it seemed to me as if she wore a mask, and what lay behind that mask might be very different from what men thought.

"As much as anyone who lopes Voor. What you have is a talent which cannot be learned, for the seeds of it are in you at birth. Though you must also stay with an elder of your kind from childhood, learning all she may teach, so that your talent is refined, as the miners reduce raw ore into metal."

"Well said," she answered. "All of it true—to a point. Only this we also know—that our healing does not work with an off-worlder, for a man, woman, or child must believe before the cure begins. While the off-worlders who visit us, even some settlers of the first generation, cannot accept what we have to offer. Therefore, a part of our talent grows out of Voor itself, has roots here and perhaps this gift has other purposes of which we are still ignorant."

"So you seek for an answer to such another purpose in the Shadow doomed places?"

"A year ago," she did not answer me directly, nor even look at me, instead turned her head a fraction so that her eyes were on the fast-falling dark and the grazing gars who were near formless bulks moving slowly in their circle about us. "I was at the holding of Bethol s'Theo—I had gone there on a call reaching me while I was beside the sea gathering the kor weed from which we make a soothing drink for the very young. Only another had been close enough to answer the calling first. She—her name was Catha and she also came from the north and from one of the Shadowed places—it was named Uthor's hold."

She paused as if expecting some word of recognition from me but I could not give it. We had visited seven of the Shadow ruins. Two had been old and even my father could not put name to them, though he grasped quickly at any hint of lore concerning such.

"The one for whom the call was made was not born in Bethol's hold, nor was his name even known. He was found on the shore after a great storm, and the belief was that he was thrown or had crawled out of the fury of the sea. Yet no one ventures out upon the sea at that season—and at other times there is no reason for going far beyond the shore with the fishing fleet—"

She was very right. On other worlds there were stretches of sea between masses of land. I had seen such configurations on the tapes my father used to teach me something of the past of our species. But Voor was different—here was one great mass of land which extended completely around the world and the two seas framing it were narrow and dangerous, rent by sudden storms which churned them into death traps. Men only traveled on land—as yet so thinly settled there was not much need for the stretching out—and there was always the Shadow menace to be feared in new places.

"His hurts of body were not so serious," Illo was continuing. "Catha laid the healing on him and those wounds closed cleanly, were beginning to renew fresh, unharmed flesh. But his mind was rent worse than any blow to a skull could have made it. So—just as she reached into the wounds to drive out the infection and bring healing, so did Catha enter his mind—"

I drew a sharp breath. There was something in me which recoiled instinctively from such an action as Illo described. Now the girl turned to me full face, and there was no longer a mask upon her features, rather her mouth was stern set, a spark shone deep in her eyes, a spark which might have been the seed of anger.

"Where there is a need, there the healer serves. Does it matter if it is a shattered body—or a shattered mind?" she demanded.

"Perhaps that is so. Still—would you if you could throw open your mind to another, make *all* your thoughts plain? I cannot believe that many would say 'yes' if you asked them that."

She sat silent for a long moment and then nodded slowly. "So one who is not a healer would answer so, to that I will agree. But minds can be healed, and if we know this to be true, then should we not also use our talent to accomplish that? Think about it, Bart s'Lorn. Would you want to go on living with a broken mind, babbling incoherently, perhaps rising to a fury which would set you to kill the innocent?

"However, Catha did try to apply to this man the healing power of the mind. I was there and I followed where I could, giving also of my strength and will. And she was succeeding," excitement had crept now into Illo's voice, "I tell you she was doing what she willed. Then—it came—a shadow, a darkness—it struck— both at the man—and at Catha—so that she herself had to withdraw swiftly into unconsciousness. The man lay screaming of monstrous things which he saw gathered around him, tormenting him. Catha remained for hours in her own withdrawal sleep. When she came again to knowledge—she was changed.

"In her there was a purpose as strong as any healing power. She knew something she would not share with us—even with me who had tried to sustain her. She went to the man and she—killed!"

I was as startled as if the Shadows came down upon us. For what Illo had said was against all right, all reason, all sanity. No healer could kill. One could use her talent to ward off physical danger—but to kill— no!

"It is true," the girl cried now as if I had denied her story. "For I saw it. She killed, and then she went out

of the holding, and she would speak to no one. Also—
there was that clinging to her as might a journey cloak
which made all whom she met turn aside and give her
room. Nor was she seen or heard of again. Until—"

"Until—" I prompted when she had been some time
silent.

"Until I dreamed. I think that she learned something in that broken mind, something of so great a horror that when it came alive or awake at her striving to
heal, it was a threat to everything which moves a
healer. She fled from it at first, and then she knew that
it had risen because of what she had tried to do and
perhaps she alone could put it to flight. So she turned
against her nature and it died. After that she must
seek—"

"For what?" I was deep into the spell of her story.
No man knows his world wholly, nor does he so know
himself. What seemed an act of blasphemy might have
been indeed one of courage as upstanding as a feast
candle flame.

"For the answer. I tried to find her for I feared that
after her act she might choose to die also. Twice I had
word of a woman seen by Voorlopers—though never
close enough that they could hail her. She was heading
north. Then—I was at Styn's Settlement where there
was a child with a broken leg and there the dream
came. I saw Catha as if she stood beside my bed, clear
and bright.

"Her face was anxious as if she faced some great
task and she looked to me. It was a calling, a true calling, though it came in a way which I never heard tell
before that a calling might. I waited two days until
I knew that the child was healing and then I started

north—"

"And you think this was all a thing connected with the Shadows?"

Illo shrugged. "How can I tell? Save the calling is still with me and it leads north. I thought first of the only Shadow doomed place I knew—that of Voor's Grove. So it was there I planned to go—but it may not be any place I yet know. And Mungo's Town was also Shadow rent."

"What do you believe this Catha is doing—or trying to do?"

"Again I do not know. Only I cannot deny her—or the calling. Have we not all long hunted some answer to the Shadow doom? Fifty planet years have those of our blood settled here. The first years—they were good —you have heard the stories of those, many times—all children listen. Then—something happened—there are no records of what it was or where the ill began. One by one the northern holds and settlements were Shadowed—died—except for such as you and I—a few children—babies—who were Voor born—who lived— but could not remember. If Catha has found a beginning or even a path which will lead to the answer—"

"Such a search is madness!" I interrupted her sharply. "You know what doom the Shadows bring—" As had my father who had also spent his life in such a search.

"Who or what are the Shadows?" She asked the same question which had lain earlier in my own mind "Did not your father ever seek answers just as Catha has done? You went willingly with him—"

"Not all the way. He would never let me enter the ruins."

"True. But all he learned there he shared with you, did he not? You see, before I dreamed I went to Portcity and there I asked access to such of his recordings as are known. He left very few there—only answers the authorities demanded from time to time. I listened, I watched. Perhaps he—and now you—know the most of any now living on Voor."

"Which is very little—no more than you could have read in the official tapes."

"Yes, and those tapes which you brought with you," she sat quietly, her hands resting palm upwards on her knees as if she mutely asked for something which could fill them.

Why had I clung to the tapes? I had told myself that they might provide us with a guide—to what? Not Mungo's, for we had never returned there. To my own private questions? I had heard them many times over and never been the wiser.

"I don't know!" My voice was over-loud; in answer I heard Witol grunt heavily out of what was now the true night darkness, as if he too questioned me in some way. "I know nothing more than the tapes."

"You were very close to your father—did he never try to awake your memory?"

"No!" my reply was as quick and hot. "He never asked—he never let the Portcity medics see me when I was little—" That much I could remember, of staying hidden in the wagon whenever we were forced, when my father could not prevent it, to visit that stronghold of the off-worlders. It had been three years or more before he took me with him into the town. In some way I understood he had feared for me. What had he known from his own days off-world that had made him so reluctant to have me questioned?

"Me they tried," she said then and there was a cold note in her voice. "They decided I was memory blocked—"

"But—but that is off-world technique!" I protested. "Do you mean that the Shadow doom is not of Voor—?"

"It is of Voor," her reply was flat. "There is probably more than one way of closing a child's memory— a small child's. Great terror can do it naturally, drugs perhaps—even interference such as one who has the healer's knowledge can use for evil. I think your father knew, or suspected something—that is what he went searching for, always protected in a safe suit. How did he even get such as that? They are not common issue on Voor where it has been generations since the First-In Scouts downed ship here and found—at that time— nothing of a menace."

"I don't know where he got it. He—he just un-packed it one day and used it."

"Used it needlessly—if his reports were correct."

"Yes."

Suddenly then her hands flew upwards, covered her ears. She bent forward as one who has a sharp pain thrust through mid-body.

"The calling!" she cried aloud. There was fear in her voice.

"Now?" I was on my feet, staring out into the dark, turning slowly.

There was no longer any crunching sound from the grazing gars. Instead I heard the thump of a hoof beating hard on the earth in half challenge, such a sound as Witol made should he meet the lead bull of another loper team—a warning as well as a recognition of the other's equal status.

"Never has it come thus before—" her voice trailed away. "We are right—our course lies ahead."

"I go only to do what my father asked of me." My voice sounded sullen in my own ears. I was not going to be drawn into her mysterious quest for a healer who had betrayed her kind by killing. I did not want to know what lay behind the wall in my memory, even if that was what *she* sought.

"Well enough—" the pain and startlement had gone out of her voice. With the moon yet to rise I could not see more of her than a formless lump on the improvised bed place. "Follow your path as I must mine, Voorloper. Still I believe that those trails are one and the same."

I heard rustling movements as if she were settling herself to sleep. Now, though still uneasy, I lay down and pulled my own blanket over me, pillowing my head on the edge of my back pack. Over me the stars were bright and clear. I thought of the off-worlders who wandered among those as we Voorlopers wander the plains of this world. *They* were pent in a ship, I lay under the open sky. If they sought strange things and mysteries to beckon them on, so did I have the same, whether I willed it so or not.

The gars had returned to grazing. Whatever had brought that warning stamp from Witol no longer seemed to trouble him. Resolutely I tried not to think of what lay on that crude sled beyond our night resting place. My father was not there—

He had never followed any formal religious practices, though he was a believer. In fact he had pointed out in his education of me that tolerance of the beliefs of others was the mark of a properly taught man, and that one did not force any faith—such must be found each by himself for himself. Yet he had believed also that this life was not the only one which a certain element within us knew. Why had he been so determined that his body be returned to the spot he had avoided all these years? Last night I had been so numbed by my loss I could not have asked those questions. Now I began to realize that what I had known of my father had been perhaps only a small portion of the real man, and that brought a hurt of its own which lay heavy in me.

I must have dreamed that night for I awoke heavy hearted—with a dull pain behind my eyes and a feeling of some danger which I had faced or had sought to face. Illo seemed in no better mood, and there was little talk between us as we broke camp and, once more taking up our burdens and apportioning theirs among the gars, went on. Though first I stepped to the top of that grass-entwined ridge and used the distance glasses.

The dark mass of the Tangle lay there right enough, still forming a low-lying cloud which met the earth at the horizon. Immediately ahead it was farther off and I guessed by comparing what I saw with the lines on my map that I had by luck, chance, or something which perhaps had greater influence than either, chosen rightly. We were headed directly towards Mungo's.

We made good time, also, for the gars fell at once into their distance-eating, long-legged stride. No large head dipped now to catch up a mouthful of grass tops

as they went. Rather Witol pressed on, the others followed, at a lumbering trot which soon made me
lengthen stride to keep up with him, making no matter
of the sled he drew and which skidded from side to
side, caught momentarily on some tuft of grass, to be
jerked free again by a slight movement of those heavy
shoulders.

The sun pushed up the sky and once or twice we
paused, drank sparingly of our water and shared part
of the second tank with the gars. Loper that I was and
used to tramping, I found that this push was greater
than I had known before. Still I had no wish to slacken

pace. If Illo was drawn by that "call," I had a similar spur within me which demanded speed and yet more speed.

In mid-afternoon we sighted with the naked eye the beginning of Mungo's ruins. Winds and rains, perhaps as punishing as the storm which had driven us across the grass lands at the height of its unleashed fury, had had their way here unchecked. Walls were rubble, the outer ramparts of the settlement looked to be no more than a tumbled hillock. There was the darker vegetation arising about it, that strange, warped vegetation which was the sign of the Shadow doom. Trees which were not wind-twisted awry, but unnaturally so wrung from their sapling birth, clung among the fallen blocks and rotted timbers.

There seemed to be more vivid life there than in the grey-brown of the plains where the grass had been bleached and aged by the sun and was now dying in the autumn chill of the night frosts. The growth marking the town was still dark, still swelling with life, as if it were encapsuled in another season. Yet the swelling plants, the crooked-trunked trees were forbidding.

Our fast forward trot slowed the closer we came to those fallen walls, that choked dark green—a green which in these sites was spotted with black in places, as if a blight-like rot fed upon it from the first moment that each leaf uncurled, and yet was never able to consume all it had fastened upon.

At length the gars stopped and the three drew together in a line, facing towards the haunted ruins. I knew their reaction of old—not one of the animals would approach such remains beyond a certain point. Only men went forward; perhaps only my species was foolish enough to venture so.

6.

I unhooked the sled ties from Witol after shucking my back-pack and freeing the other gars from their burdens. Illo helped in my task without breaking the silence which had fallen between us when we at last sighted my goal. She had said it was hers also—but I determined that the venture which I had sworn to carry out would be mine alone.

Though I had viewed those other ruins my father had prospected down the years and this looked no different, still it was the one which had been my own birthplace, in which I had lived, where something unbelievable had happened. I was frankly afraid, still I knew that I must pass that fear if I could not overcome it.

At last I faced the girl squarely.

"This," I said with all the force I could summon, trying so hard to make my voice have the unyielding authority my father knew so well how to summon, "I must do alone."

I had so much expected a protest from her that I was oddly deflated when she stepped back a pace, plainly joining with the uneasy gars, and answered me:

"This is for you, yes."

I took the cords of the sled in my hands, put all the strength I could muster into drawing the burden behind me as I turned away abruptly to face the sprawling sore which had once been a settlement of my own kind, and in which lurked the unknown which all the beliefs of Voor made out to be our greatest enemy. Night was not too far off and I wanted to have done with my task before the dark closed in, though I had my torch ready to hand, newly furnished with a fresh unit.

It took both strength and will to pull my burden on. I did not look back, rather narrowed and concentrated all my energy and thought on one thing—the speedy fulfilling of the promise I had made. The closer I approached what had been Mungo's Town the more something deep within me fed the beginning of panic. Only that I dared not acknowledge. More than the stubborn weight and heaviness of the sled made me breathe quickly, as a man pants in a grueling race. I set my teeth and pulled viciously, until the cords bit into my wrists and hands, and found that small pain was steadying.

The vegetation did not present too thick a barrier— in fact there was a kind of opening directly ahead of me, as if at one time or other the growth had been cut back to clear a path. Though the very suggestion that that had been done was enough to feed my uneasiness. I had no choice with my bulky and awkward burden but to make that gap my entrance.

The fleshy growth was even less natural looking close by. A small branch I had to fend away broke with

ing free its plug with my teeth I splashed the contents over my burned skin, taking more in the palm of my unburned hand to fling at the fiery torment on my jaw and throat. Easement came almost as quickly as the pain had struck.

Get out—that was a shout filling my mind now—get out!

I kicked about me to clear a path ahead and my efforts uncovered what had brought me down. A blaster lay there, its metal pitted with holes, though it had not been eaten by rust. Another kick sent the weapon flying back into concealment, I pulled at the thongs, and was out into the wide space around the hall.

Here alone there were no dancing flower heads, no acid-sapped vegetation. Instead— I stood staring in disbelief. If such had been in those other ruins my father had described on tapes, he had not been able to mention it.

For what I was looking at was bones—skeletons huddled together along the walls of the hall. Almost as if the whole village had been lined up by a ruthless enemy and blasted down all at one time. Such signs of violent death were difficult to comprehend for a moment—though I had seen death before, but never a slaughter on such a scale. There were no signs of the bleached bones of blaster fire which was my only knowledge of any weapon which could hit so widely and suddenly as to wipe out a whole village.

I forced myself to move forward. There were no other relics visible. The ground under them was barren earth, unmarked by any scorching. Metal objects, a buckle, the hooks on any settler's belt—even perhaps

an ornament—nothing of such showed—

The bodies lay in some order. Had they been gathered so by a survivor? Only as far as I knew *I* had been the only survivor and no five-year-old child could arrange this. Had my father, perhaps someone else who had returned later, arranged the dead in such a manner—but why?

I worked my way around that line of bones, and, taking out my hand torch, entered the hall itself. Perhaps the answer could be found here. In spite of the open window spaces, the vanished door, it was dim within until I turned my torch to full and began a slow sweep about the room.

There were benches, in rows covered with dust. At the far end of the room a platform one step high had given a stage of sorts. I knew that this was like all village halls—it was the center of education, of entertainment, of the necessary meetings to discuss common policy. There was nothing here—

I stumbled a little as I went back into the open. The night was coming fast. I was filled with a need to be

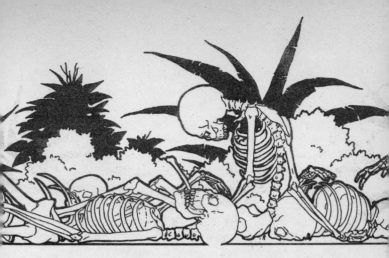

free, out of Mungo's Town before darkness fell. There were shadows gathering— Shadows!

What *was* the Shadow Doom? Who had first called the menace so? That one must have known *something* to be able to impart a name to the danger. I walked closer now along the line of unknown dead. There were only bones—twice I noted smaller skeletons which must have been children. Why had they died and I survived?

This did not look like the result of a plague—then the unburied dead would have been found in their houses. No, this more resembled an execution!

That thought arose against my fear. For an execution meant an enemy—one which or who must have form and substance, who could be fought—made to pay! Was this what had ridden my father all through the years? Had he come back to look upon the dead and guess—likewise guess enough so that he spent the rest of his life in search?

Yet he had found nothing, and he had been closer to the actual outrage than I was now. If he had only told me more! My blistered hand hurt as I formed a fist. I needed badly a spur for definite action, for a chance to fight back.

Instead I turned at the end of the row of the dead and went back to the sled. I pulled this onto the barren earth where even my own boots had left no track. Carefully I lined up that improvised transport and its sealed burden with the rest who lay there.

For the first time I wondered if my father had had another reason to send me here—not just to return him to lie among those with whom he had had some tie in years past—(which of those skeletons might be my mother? I flinched from that thought as if it were a blow). No, could it be that he meant me to confront the horror which had happened here and react just as I was doing, determining that, when he had been forced to relinquish the search, I would take it up? If that were so—then he was succeeding. Though I had heard of the Shadow Doom all my life, had seen its effect on my father and others, it had never been as real to me as it was at this moment.

I hurried back the way marked by the torn vegetation, wanting to be out of the town. Still I was certain that I would return—I had to know! For the first time I could share with Illo the demands of her own search—if the woman she sought, this healer named Catha, could give me any answers, then those I must have!

Illo had not been idle while I was gone. She had established a small camp at the nearest point the gars would advance towards the village, even hacking off armloads of the grass to form such beds as those we had rested upon the night before. The spread of the ever-present plains grass was not as thick, nor did it grow so tall here. There was evidence that these had once been fields and straggling through the choking grass, putting up a valiant battle for growing room, were clumps of grain now harvest yellow.

Though the gars were at graze, devouring such clumps with greedy relish, I noted that they followed the pattern they always had used when we were encamped near ruins. Two would eat for a space, the third stand with head up and pointed towards the remains of the town. Though they exchanged the post of sentry through such timing and selection they appeared to agree upon among themselves, there was one ever on watch.

I quickened pace as I saw the loads piled and Illo's work. The blisters on my skin were once more smarting and I wanted her verdict on my hurts. She was swift to see my injuries, and, when I told her how they had occurred, she searched her pack to bring forth a pot of greenish ointment which, after she had washed the blisters carefully once more with water, she spread over the burns leaving them free from pain with the redness of the skin beginning slowly to fade

Water was our need. We had that which had been carried in the wagon containers on gar back but it was not enough to last long for both the animals and ourselves. The settlement must have had some close and well-enduring source of water. Though that would have been pumped through pipes into the ruins (and I, for one, would not set to my lips any liquid which bubbled within that place of death) still the ultimate source should be beyond the village itself. I summoned Witol with my whistle and he came to me, a generous wisp of the grain stalks bobbing from his moving jaws.

It was well known that gars could scent water where a man with his inferior senses could easily die of thirst, and what I asked of the lead bull now he had done many times before. Letting him scent the liquid left in my canteen I made the hand signal for "seek." After a moment of rumination, he swallowed his mouthful and began to trot to the east purposefully.

I took Illo's canteen and one of the wagon cans—it now being light enough that I could carry it. We crossed the lines of more grown over fields where I could trace irrigation ditches, the kind used in plains settlements during the dry months of mid-summer. Witol held up his head, his nostrils wide open. Now he uttered a grunt from deep within his throat as we came upon what had once been a reservoir. The soil had been dug away and the deep pocket left, spread with several coatings of plasta, made a smooth bowl which cupped now enough water to reflect the sunset, and ran in a small stream through an underground duct which I believed entered the village.

The source was partly rain and what else arose from a spring occupying an opening in the plasta on the side away from the ruins. I kicked off my boots so that I might better walk over the slick of the plasta and went to fill the containers, Witol drinking noisily from the pool. The water was cool near the spring and sweet. Since the gar showed no repulsion I could believe it good.

I had been so immersed in my own thoughts since I had come out of Mungo's that I hardly realized that Illo and I had said very little to one another. Save that I had described to her the plants which had led to the poison effect on my skin, some necessary exchanges concerning matters of our camp, we had not spoken together. However, when I returned with the water container full resting on Witol's back, and twilight thickened, I resolved that I must tell her of my discovery.

That night we dared a fire. There was no time in the past when there had appeared to be any danger beyond the ruins, as I could testify from my own experience, and anything stalking prey on the plains would not come near one of the Shadow-taken settlements. There is something about fires, that earliest weapon of our species against the power of darkness, which provides us with a comfort to the spirit as well as the body. Looking into the flames I could even imagine that all I had seen that day was part of a dream. Since that was not so Illo must have a full accounting.

I spoke stiffly, bluntly, with an attempt at preserving a lack of emotional involvement. The bones, white, stripped, nameless could not convey to me as much of an impact that bodies would have. When I finished my story, my companion in this quest was quiet for a long moment. Then she asked, as if it was something she must do, though she hated the need:

"You—you knew none? There was no return of memory?"

"Nothing—I—" my hesitation was of a space of a breath only, "I looked—there was nothing, not even a bit of metal to identify one from the other. Though I think that all the villagers must have been there. Why not me? I saw what must have been other children—"

Her face wore that impassive mask-like look. "How old would you guess?"

I moved uneasily. "I could not say—none were very small."

"And you were five," she mused aloud. "I must have been nearly four—there were two who were babies—and one woman—but she was brain hurt and disappeared into the Tangle. She broke the bonds the medics laid upon her and they later tracked her to that."

"But the babies—what became of them?"

She cupped her chin in her hand, rested the elbow of that arm upon her knee where she sat on a pack of the gear we had not needed to open. It seemed that she, too, looked now into the fire for comfort.

"Brother and sister—twins. They had a kinsman who was off-world and who had come with the thought of staying at Voor's Grove. When he heard what had happened he took them and shipped out. I never heard what happened to them after."

"There were eight settlements and holdings in all which were overrun," I totalled them up on my fingers. "Mungos, Voors—Stablish's in the far west and, a little south of that, an off-worlder one, only that was not a real settlement, rather a semi-permanent station set up to study vegetation cross-breeding. Then eastward, Welk's Town, Lomack's, Robbin's, Kattern's. We, my father and I, went to Welk's, Lomack's, Kattern's, the off-world station and Stablish's. How many others had survivors—children?"

"Why—" her mask cracked and her eyes showed a flicker of astonishment. "Only—only you and I! That is all. You know, of course, of the birth lag—"

That had been another peculiarity of Voor which I had half forgotten over the years since my father had

had me read the records. The birth lag—colonists were encouraged to have children as soon as possible if the conditions on the settled world were favorable. But on Voor there had been a strange effect which had at first caused some concern, and then, as the years passed, and more settlers came, had been accepted as the norm for this world. No children had been born during the first six years after landing. Then an established pattern of cycle births, for there would be a few years in which the number of births was approximately normal for our species on the home planets from which they had come. Again would follow birth lags of increasingly shorter intervals. Until now that oddity did not exist—at least not in the south. And since no one settled in the north now, if it still differed that did not matter.

"What if ages five or six—and under—meant immunity—" Illo continued. "You may have been the youngest—the latest born at Mungo Town. I was the first of another grouping at Voor's. We have never known what caused the lag—just as we don't know what caused that—" She pointed through the twilight to the settlement. "All the other settlements and holdings could have been caught by chance during the long lag—so no survivors."

Her reasoning made sense. Then our own chance of survival had indeed been very small; we were the only two of our kind. Whether that could mean anything or not, I was in no position to argue.

"What are you going to do now?"

I knew, though I had not yet put my resolve into words. "Try to find out."

That had become the future for me. I could return to

Portcity, yes—start over as a loper, back-packing on my three remaining gars—making the rounds as a small trader. Or I could join some holding—an extra pair of hands was welcome anywhere on the frontier. But I would not. I *had* to know—if such a thing was possible to learn at all.

The girl regarded me steadily. "Your father had years of searching—what did he learn? You may be running now into something worse that you can remember—because you don't remember!"

I thought of those ordered rows of the dead within the town—the suggestion in that of a reason, a definite pattern behind this depopulation of the north. There was something utterly dark and cruel in the way those bones lay along the wall—something I could not live with in my memory.

"They were killed, deliberately, for some purpose. It wasn't an illness, or animals in attack, or—" I tried to reckon up the dangers which could wipe out a town. "The Survey reports all say that Voor has no intelligent life above the 6-plus level. If there has been a Jack outfit in hiding here that would have recorded, no matter how many distorts they tried to use. Even a distort records—something."

Illo shook her head. The firelight flickered, sometimes seeming to make her eyes show with a spark of fire of their own, or so it seemed to me. I wanted to look at her just because she was alive, clothed in flesh, able to talk, to think, to be—not like that— I tried to shut down hard on the picture which kept creeping out of the dark into some line of vision which was in my mind and not directly before my eyes.

"All of those explanations—they have been worn

into tatters." She raised one hand and brushed back a wisp of hair from her forehead. "None of them, except perhaps a plague, would account for the radical change in vegetation. I know herbs, most of the wild grasses, the plants. The knowledge is part of my training. This afternoon, while you were gone, I went close enough to view what grows over there. It is all different —it reminds me of the Tangle in some ways—still it is not of that either. It is poisoned—you have your own experience with it to prove that." She gestured at my hand, shiny with the balm she had spread over it.

"What about you—your calling?"

She shook her head. "It—it is gone."

"What do you mean?"

"Just that. And I have never known a calling to end so before. I think—I think she is dead—."

"Your Catha?"

"Yes." The single word brought silence.

"So you will go back then? I can give you Wobru— a water tank—"

"No!" Her word of denial was emphatic as that "yes" had been earlier. "I must know—just as you must. There is some reason why we survived—"

"You said it yourself—by chance we were the right age."

"Beside that." She made an impatient gesture with one hand. "You are not a true believer, are you?"

"A true believer in what?"

"One of the Assembly of the Spirits," her voice was as impatient as her gesture had been.

"No. But surely you aren't either." I knew the Assembly—they occupied three settlements in the south, keeping very much to themselves and having only necessary contact with others. Their lives were narrow, ruled by what my father had termed "taboos." His own acceptance of differences between men had been very liberal and his distrust of fanaticism had led him to impress upon me the fact that some of the worst disasters in the history of our species have been born from judging strangers by standards we held too rigidly. In my father's eyes there was a simple code of right and wrong which guided any man. And he had acknowledged some power beyond our knowledge at work in the universe.

The Assembly in their rigid beliefs were, as the miners and other stations manned by off-worlders, the few places not welcoming healers. That she would mention them now startled me.

"No," she agreed. "I am not one of them. How could I be, as you say? But they have certain interesting beliefs—such as the one that we are intended for specific roles in life, and, from what is so, ordained, we cannot escape. We may deliberately turn aside from a road because we dislike what it entails for us, yet the side turning we choose will eventually curve back to bring us to the same end. In this matter—"

"That is *their* belief!" I countered. "It is only chance that you and I are survivors—there is no mysterious 'spirit' or fate guiding us along." That was one idea I would not allow myself to accept. The decision which I had come to in Mungo's when I had seen that open graveyard had not been dictated to me; it was my own, or rather one I had taken up because of the man who had been the center of my world. Whatever had left the sign of its—or their—cruel passing must be made to answer—if it was humanly possible to make this so.

In a way, though I believed in her story of Catha and the calling which had brought her to join us, I was glad that Illo was not to be our guide now. I accepted what I could see, hear, touch— I was not a healer, and if I were to succeed in finding the murderers of Mungo's it must be by my own senses and not depending on something which was not a part of me.

"You believe in yourself?" Her question cut through my thoughts and surprised me.

"As much as I can." I was honest with her. I had never really been placed on my own before, I realized that. Any decision I made now, any mistake in judgment or action, would be my own and I must face the results alone.

"That was a fair answer," Illo nodded. "So do I also. I believe in my own training and say this much— we are meant to do this thing. Also, though the calling has failed, we should still point north. You returned to Mungo's and have made one discovery there which your father has not recorded. I say now let us go to Voor's Grove— No," she did not give me any time to protest. "Your story began here and returning has seemed of little use in unraveling it. Do not deny me the chance to return to *my* beginning; perhaps we may profit from it more than you can now guess.

I had to admit that I had no other goal, and surely I could learn little more from Mungo's. Why not agree? Voor's Grove also my father had not visited, there was just a chance—

So I agreed because I had nothing else to offer.

7.

That night I was not ready for sleep. Instead I unpacked the reader and my father's tapes. Though I had heard them all before—some many times, for when we were on the plains he oftentimes took out one or another and sat listening to his own words relayed, a frown of concentration on his face as if he must always bolster memory, make sure that there was no clue he had perhaps overlooked. Yes, I had heard them before, but now it was my turn to concentrate, to strive to find a loose thread that I might pull on to reduce this tangled web to order.

Illo listened with the same absorption. We heard descriptions of just such plants as I had encountered that afternoon—of the fact that, though the buildings on the perimeter of each deserted site had seemed to be in very bad condition, those farther in did not show the same signs of erosion. I waited eagerly for some mention of a central hall, or any indication that my father had found there evidences of massacre such as was at Mungo's. But there was nothing at all which suggested that he had ever discovered the remains of a single body.

If he had done so, why had he registered all else in minute detail and left what was a most important discovery unvoiced? There was something else—

Though he had spoken of the alien-seeming vegetation in detail, he had never described the nodding flowers. I played each tape to the end as the red moon climbed the night sky. The gars had come closer to the fire. Wobru and Bru were lying down, chewing their cuds rhythmically, but Witol was on his feet and disappeared at intervals. I knew that the bull was on sentry go and that I could trust his senses farther than my own.

"You have learned anything?" Illo asked as the last of the tapes came to an end.

"This much—if there were skeletons in other places my father did not mention them—or the flowers—"

"Flowers?" she pounced upon that. "What kind of flowers?"

I described the blossoms and how they had seemed to move though there was no wind. It was a small thing, but how could I rank the importance of any hint?

"They moved—" she repeated. "Bart, have you been to the Tangle edge?"

"No closer than this place. There was never any reason to head that way."

"But you have seen the picture tapes taken by Survey, by the off-world teams after the Shadow doom began?"

"Thick, grey, just what men name it—a tangle of vegetation too massed to get through except by burning. Even that does not work—the stuff is said to grow overnight and if one ventures in too far the trail closes up behind him. It dampens out coms and range fingers. They will not operate near it. That's why no one can go in—" I summoned up my general knowledge of the Tangle as I had heard and tape-read.

"Also—it moves," she said then. "As your flowers in the town—it quivers and sways even if there is no wind. That is part of the tangling process, for in its ever movement it twines and winds stem and leaf together, sometimes to remain so tied permanently."

That I had *not* known. At my questioning she said she had once been in Portcity and had heard the report of a man who had been sent on a rescue mission. Some off-worlders in a flitter had flown too low over that trap and had vanished into it.

"I wonder," she sat now with forefinger to her lips as if she would chew upon it, as one did upon a sliver of journey food, "can there be an alliance?"

"No one would be fool enough to bring seeds or plants from the Tangle to bed on the plains!"

"Perhaps no one brought them. Remember the storm? What could the force of a wind such as that carry in it? I wish there was some detailed record from one of the doomed villages of what happened just *before* the Shadows. Could there have been some signs of approaching trouble which no one thought to notice—"

"Such as a new flower popping up in a garden plot?" I wanted to scoff, yet still I was caught by her reasoning. Perhaps my father had had a somewhat similar idea; he had spent so much time in the tapes describing the vegetation. Also now I remembered something else—that when he wore the protect suit he had always shed that well away from the camp site and had brushed it over with disfect powder. But that

133

had been for the first two or three times he had gone so exploring; after that he had not even used the suit.

"Such as a flower, a new flower, in a garden place," she agreed.

Illo knew more of growing things than I did, that I was willing enough to allow. A healer must have a wide knowledge of plants, which harm and which can help. I knew that in her pack she had small boxes of dried leaves, of crushed-to-powder seeds—all of which had their uses. While the blisters still on my hand and cheek, though they had lost the sting of pain under Illo's treatment, were warning enough that poison grew and flourished in Mungo's. At this moment I was ready to open my mind to any theory. Though I could not equate any inimical plant with what I had seen. Poison in such might produce a plague, yes. But I was still certain that there was some cruel thought behind the doom. Perhaps not thought as we reckoned it—still intelligence, however alien that might be in form.

I packed away the tapes and we both lay down on our grass and blanket beds. Illo had said very little, but I guessed that she was thinking much. I hoped I would not keep seeing, even in dreams, that which lay so close to us behind the nodding flowers. Did they still nod at night, I wondered? This was so still a night, without even a breath of wind stirring in the grass. As if something lay behind its defenses in the dead town —waiting— No, I must not allow my imagination to stray so.

It was a restless night for me. I must have slept very lightly for twice I roused to hear the gars changing watch. I realized that night not how much I knew, but how little. I had thought that I was well equipped for a Voorloper—yet now I needed more—so much more.

The gars were brisk in setting out the next day, glad in their own way, I was certain, that we were turning our backs upon a place they shunned. Witol now car-

ried the water cans filled to their cap pieces, while Bru was free of burden. She took to ranging ahead, criss-crossing our chosen direction of march. It was as if she were playing scout. I had never seen a gar behave so before, but then, mainly, they had marched in yoke with the wagon and not gone ranging free on the trail.

There was no trail in the grass to be sure. The sky today was overcast. I kept watch on the scudding clouds. Another bad storm might well mean our deaths when we had not even the shelter of the wagon. However, the animals showed no signs of uneasiness, and I knew that they would betray those well ahead of a drastic natural change.

To the right that distant threat of the Tangle marked the horizon line; we were heading due west in the general direction of Voor's Grove as well as I could place it. By all accounts that would be yet two days journey away.

There were formations of migrating birds across the sky and their cries reached us above the constant rustle of the grass which made up part of the wind's song. Our pace was steady but we did not push, as now and then we rested while the gars grazed. We did not talk even when we so paused. Illo wore her mask face and I had an eerie feeling that I, the gars, perhaps even the plain over which we trode, was not really visible to her, that she was deep somewhere within herself working out some problem. At our third rest I dared to ask her if she had picked up her call again. She shook her head.

"There is nothing. Perhaps I shall never know—" her voice trailed away and I could add the missing words for myself. She would never know what had happened to Catha. I guessed, though I did not say so, that what had come was death.

In mid-afternoon I sighted a small herd of lurts—the first life other than winged we had seen since the storm. The natural inhabitants of the plains must have gone to cover then or else were so scattered and mauled that they had been driven from their regular territories. Witol bellowed and the small graceful creatures fled in great bounds. We do not know why the gars will warn off the wild grazers—perhaps they have a kind of jealous desire to protect food which they might just need.

However the sight of the lurts running free meant that this was truly a deserted land. The most timid of creatures, they would not even share territory with other wildlife larger than themselves.

"This is good country." We had paused at the top of one of the low ridges. Illo shifted her pack a fraction and then went down on one knee and parted the heavy growth of grass. I thought she was looking at the richness of the soil, but instead she dug a moment with her fingers among the grass roots and then held up something which caught glittering life from the daylight as it swung back and forth in her grasp.

"This—have you seen its like before? You have ranged far—" She held her find out to me.

There was a chain of metal links. At first I thought that exposure had given it that bronze-blue color. Only when I took it from her, it was not pitted, and I believed that the smooth surface was not in the least touched by time. If that were its natural color the material was like nothing I had ever seen. Which meant little—it could have been dropped by some off-

worlder, perhaps a prospector, the metal forming it an alloy from another world.

The chain was beautifully fashioned, a work of art, the links fastened one to another as the scales of a sku lizard are set on the skin. It was broken, but mid-point along its length, when it had been intact and the clasp locked, there was a plate set in as part of the chain, curved a little to continue the line it must hold to fit closely about the throat. That plate was about the width and length of my shortest finger, and, as I wiped it clear of the remains of the soil from which Illo had freed it, I could see that it was deeply incised with a bewilderingly ornate scrolling which resembled somehow an unknown script.

"Off-world," I commented. I peered around at the grassy slopes which descended gently from where we stood. Perhaps it was my experience in Mungo's but I found myself hunting for some sign, unpleasant, of whoever had once worn it. I would not have been surprised to see a skull peering open-eyed at me from behind one of the tussocks.

"Perhaps—" She sat back on her heels and set about dividing the grass, pulling at it. Was she also hunting such grim remains? If the same thought which nibbled at me struck her I wondered that she still explored so.

"This is an alloy—I think." I wanted her to stop that search. "We have no art, no skill to produce such a thing on Voor."

"It is older than the coming of Voor—" Her search had proved fruitless. She looked up, not to me, but at what I held.

"You mean it dates back before the coming of Survey—?" Voor had been the First-In Scout who had mapped this planet for the League and because he had been close to retirement, on his last out-range of exploration, it had been given his name. He had chosen to settle here when his service years were ended.

"Yes."

"But that is impossible!" I twirled the chain between my fingers and was surprised that she would make such a statement. Or why—

She wiped the last of the earth traces from her fingers and arose.

"You know little about us—the healers." There was affront in her voice, her lips were thin set and her eyes were as unfriendly as if I had shouted "Liar!" at her openly. "We have gifts. I—and several others of my craft—can hold a wrought object thus," she set her palms together with exaggerated gesture, a little cupped as if the chain did so lie in her grasp, "and know what a thing is in truth—something of its age, of those who made it, used it—perhaps even how it reached where it lay until I saw it."

I would have denied that this could be done, then I hesitated. Who knew what could be done truly with the mind? There were off-world strains who had odd gifts. Terran blood had mutated and changed as those from the home planet reached out to the stars, found rooting on distant worlds, developed from the use of alien soils and atmosphere changes which grew ever stronger, became a more permanent part of each generation under those foreign suns. Though I had never been off-world, I had seen enough of the many types (and those were only a very small number who ever made Voor a landfall) at Portcity, visitors, members of

the commissions come to investigate the doom, miners, starmen, to understand that we, who had common ancestors long ago, were now sometimes different species altogether. There were also those who had never been human by our small standards at all—the Zacathans, the Trystians—others.

So it was never wise to state absolutely that this or that talent could not exist. Even the settlers of Voor had come from several different worlds and so had bloodlines which might have branched untold planet years back, giving their descendents unusual attributes.

"Let me psyche—" She took the chain deftly out of my hold, did indeed cup it between her hands. Her eyes were closed, I could see her whole body tense in the act of complete concentration.

I had felt nothing save the smooth surface of the chain. Though the idea clung to my mind that the scrolling on that foreplate did have a definite and important meaning—almost as if it were an identity disc such as are worn by starmen in some services.

An identity disc? Not impossible. There could even have been a ship's crash—or the coming of a single LB, escaping from some catastrophe in space before Voor made this world his last official landfall. That fitted plausably. Only that would put back the age at least a century, perhaps more. No metal or alloy I know of could have existed uneroded—unless—

Forerunner!

We are late comers into space, even though we have been for centuries now star voyagers. Still there had been those who had sought the star lanes, mapped and held them, long before our first crude rocket had lifted from Terra and man had eyed the stars with a covetous desire. Galactic empires had risen and fallen and of them we knew so little.

The Zacathans had their records. In their long lives (so much longer than the years any of us might aspire to) they had made it their purpose to search out, to catalogue all of the alien remains which could be found. There had been many such finds—the Caves of Astra, the half-melted and blasted cities on Limbo— even greater discoveries. Machines so intricate and obtuse that our best trained techs could not begin to understand them. Some had kept on running, even on deserted worlds—for how long—a million years—a billion?

I remembered my father's other abiding interest, the gathering of such material on Forerunner finds as trickled through to the records of Portcity, his stories at our lonely campfires of what had been found—and how we had only barely touched the edge of that knowledge which the forerunners had lived with for eons. However, there were no known Forerunner ruins here—or at least none which had been discovered.

It was easy to build and speculate on such a hint. We had our First-In Scouts—perhaps the Forerunners had had such explorers also. One had landed on Voor —or whatever name he had given this world in his turn —come to trouble in some fashion and—

Illo's face broke the mask which fell on her when she withdrew into her healer's trance. It twisted as if she were in some actual pain and with a sudden movement she hurled the chain from her. I gave a cry of half protest and fell on my knees, scrabbling through the grass with my hands until my fingers found that smooth length.

The girl had not yet opened her eyes, but her tormented expression appeared to intensify. She shivered so violently that she near over-balanced and did waver from one side to the other, until, having reclaimed her find, I reached her side and threw my arm about her shoulders, drawing her close until I could steady her against my own body. I could feel still that shivering of —fear—revulsion—?

She raised her hands and covered her face. Now she was sobbing, harsh, hurting cries like those of an animal in pain. I heard an answering deep lowering from Witol, bellows from Bru and Wobru. The gars gathered beyond the slight rise on which we stood, their horned heads raised as they stared at us with their large eyes.

"Illo—what is it?" Perhaps some of the warmth of my body, the quiet soothing I strove very hard to put into my voice, reached her.

She lowered one hand, caught fiercely at my arm with a grip so hard that her nails bit through the leather of my sleeve so that I could actually feel pain in the flesh beneath. There were no tears on her cheek; though her breath came in those ragged, breast-tearing sobs, her eyes were now open—and dry. She stared straight before her and there was a look about her as if she were in truth being drawn away in some terrifying fashion, that though I held her and had not and would not let go, still she was leaving me.

Dropping the chain once more to the ground I seized her by both upper arms. I shook her with what was close to a brutal assault. Her head wobbled back and forth on her shoulders. She gasped, cried out.

Only that sobbing dwindled, now she did not move to shake off my hold. Instead she took a stumbling step closer, her arms came up about my body and she held to me as tightly as if I were the only safeguard against being swept away by some peril I could neither see nor understand.

For a very long moment we stood thus. Her shivering lessened, her head had fallen forward against my shoulder, and I heard her ragged, forced breathing growing less urgent, more normal.

For the second time now I dared ask:

"What is it?"

For a second or two I was afraid that my question was going to arouse once more whatever inner storm had gripped her. She did shiver, and her hold on me tightened. Then she raised her head. Her mouth trembled but somehow she mastered whatever force had so rent her.

"I was—I was—" she shook her head in a small helpless movement as if she could summon no words to explain what had happened in that space of time which she had held the necklet and tried to understand any secret it might know.

"They—" she began again, "they did not think—think as we do. My head—it was as if someone ran through my head opening doors—letting out all kinds of things—things I could not understand—that I never knew that I could contain. It all came at once! Bart—whoever wore that—there was some terrible danger and he—she—it—" She shook her head from side to side. "I don't even know what *it* was!" Her voice was near a wail. "But there was fear—terrible fear which ate—ate right into me. And—how one who was like us

—even like— If I could only have understood, had time—it moved so fast—"

She loosed her hold on me with one hand and put it to her forehead. "So fast—and I could not follow its thoughts—they were like the flash of blaster flame—hurting—eating—in my head. But something happened here or near here—when that was dropped. And it was bad—worse than we, any of us being as we are, can understand."

Though she did not seem able to make better sense than that, the words she did find to attempt to explain steadied her. She loosed her hold on me utterly and I saw her self possession return as she spoke. She looked down to where the necklet lay.

"Bart—I dare not touch that again. But it has a message—we—someone with more training or talent than I—could understand—unravel. It is important, that much I know. Can you carry it?"

I stooped and picked it up for the second time. In my hands it was nothing but a loop of strange metal bearing, part way down its broken length, that curved bar. I felt nothing but the smooth surface. And I said so. Illo nodded.

"Put it away—safely. When—if—we get back to Portcity that must be sent off-world—to one of the League centers for sensitive learning where they have the trained handlers who deal with Forerunner things. It may be one of the keys such as men have always longed to find—if it is given to the right person who has a mind trained and safeguarded well enough to be able to put it to use."

I coiled the chain into a small ball and stowed it in my belt pouch. She watched me fasten the loop of that closely as if wishing to make very sure that her discovery would be safe. How much of what she believed was the truth I could not tell. But that she thought it was correct I had no doubts at all.

We left that ridge and tramped on, the gars scattered back into their usual line of march, no longer watching us as intently as they had when Illo had tried to learn the secret of the thing. Neither of us spoke of it, yet I was oddly aware with every stride I took of the rub of the purse back and forth against my thigh, and of what lay within it.

I had to keep a tight curb upon my tongue for I wanted very much to question her. Perhaps, I told myself, such questions might even be good, helping her to sort out whatever stream of wild impressions had overcome her. Yet it was not right, I thought, to put her to such a task now—not unless she opened the subject. Which she did not do.

Once more we camped on the plains. This time with no fire, since we were out of the range of the ruins which had a certain "safe" area about them—no animals venturing any nearer than our gars would go. It was the gars who again played sentry for us. Illo was not silent this night. Instead she talked almost feverishly, as if she must hear the sound of voices— using that sound as a barrier against something else.

She spoke of her wanderings as a healer—she seemed to have ranged distances by choice rather than settled long at any hold or settlement—going up along the coast, striking inland—visiting Portcity to renew certain supplies and talk with ships' medics. For offworlders though those were, they were more keenly interested in any planet form of medicine and healing than the mine medics. She said that many of them compiled records of unusual healing processes from world to world—and she had found them most willing to tell her what they could of worlds where there were also healers not unlike herself in training—people who could diagnose illness often by touch alone and subdue pain and conquer disease by drawing it out of the body by their wills.

That she had an inquiring mind I already knew, but now I saw that she had a deep thirst for knowledge, save that as all healers it was not a knowledge which depended upon machines and technology, but rather upon what lay within a man or woman—dormant sometimes—to be tapped by those lucky or learned

enough to be able to open the right door.

The right door—what she had said about that feeling in her brain when she had tried to psyche the chain returned to me. Opened doors with that behind them spilling out in no pattern which she could understand. Such a thing—it could lead to madness. I resolved in that moment that if it were possible I would never let her touch the chain again. She had been strong enough this time to throw it from her before the chaos it bred in her mind had conquered. There might come another time when her thirst for the unknown would lead her to a second try and she could not again be as strong-willed or fortunate.

8.

Voor's Grove indeed lay in the shadow of the Tangle. It surprised me that, knowing, as they must have done, the sinister qualities of that menacing wilderness, the settlers here had drawn so close to such impenetrable mystery. Or perhaps in the days when the settlement had been first decided upon the Tangle was not considered such a menace, that men believed they might fire or dig it out of their way, altering the land as they had done successfully on other worlds.

Also, since the abandonment of the settlement, the Tangle may have grown unchecked, but then that result would differ from what had happened elsewhere. For in past years a careful check upon it had shown the growth to be static, that it neither expanded in summer seasons or retracted when the plains droughts and frosts hit hard, as they did in a regular cycle of planet weather.

Plainly Voor's Grove had been well situated as far as its founders, unaware of the Shadow doom, had decided. It lay at the uniting of two rivers—those which came together to form the greater flood of the Halb as it flowed east and south. One of these streams reached westward and north—the other came directly from the northern mounts, breaking from under the curtain of the Tangle as no other that I knew of did.

River trade in the plains lands might have built up well—had the dream of settlements here not been broken. Unfailing water in the dry years was a thing to be prized. The settlement had been placed on the vee of land where the two rivers boiled on to their uniting.

That water which flowed from the west came with a swifter current and was fairly clear. But that of the second stream moved far more slowly and was turgid, brownish and opaque. I remembered the armored thing which had been storm washed to the wagon and I would not have ventured to ford that stream no matter how shallow it measured.

Luckily there was no need to venture into what might be a water trap. There had been a bridge once, built of the same stone, brought in from the mountain quarries to the west, which formed the walls of the ruins. Enough of that span remained to give us footing.

Voor's Grove itself, even though thickly cloaked by the same poisonous-appearing vegetation as Mungo's had been, was, I could see, much the larger settlement. It was older, too, by about ten years, and had been meant by its ambitious founders to be the capital of the plains lands—hence its name.

Once more the gars would not come near, halting well away as Illo and I approached the tumbled, water-washed stones of what had once been the bridge. For all its greater size it presented the same picture of ruins and growth gone wild as had the settlement in which I had been born. I studied my companion carefully as she surveyed what we could see.

"No memories?" I could not help asking, for she was frowning as one might who was attempting to recall something which remained as only a trace at the very edge which thought could reach.

She shook her head instead of answering me, but now she moved with some purpose. Shucking her back pack she opened it and searched among the contents to bring out a skin bag which I had already seen—from which she had taken the salve which had brought me relief from the poisonous sap. She opened that and, dipping in two finger tips, brought out a gob which she proceeded to rub over her face and then both of her hands. When she had done she looked at me.

"This will save us from another accident such as you faced in Mungo's Town—"

Save—us? Then she expected me to accompany her into Voor's Grove. Perhaps for a second or two I thought of refusing, but I could not. My curiosity was far too aroused. Would we find the same signs of a massacre here?

I rubbed away until those portions of my skin which would be exposed were well covered with a film of grease carrying an odd but not unpleasant scent. It had drawn the pain from my blisters which were fast healing so they showed now only as reddish marks.

I dropped my pack beside hers and checked my belt equipment. There were tangler and stunner, both of which were fresh charged, my long knife, the pouch in which rode that enigma we had discovered in the grass, my torch—though it was still early afternoon and we should not be so long in there that I would use that. Yes, all the defenses any loper could carry were close to my hand.

Relieving the gars of their burdens, we stacked that packed gear at a point directly opposite the remains of the bridge and then set out to see what might lie within Voor's. Illo took the lead, moving out while I steaded the water carriers against the other gear, before I could call to her to wait.

She balanced lightly and skillfully from one stone to the next, twice having to jump to cross gaps in the masonry. The brown water swirling below had an oily look to it, as if it were not really water but the exudation of some unpleasant growth. I watched it carefully before I began the crossing. There was no movement to be sighted on the surface or under it. However the tumble of stones could well give good footing to any such monster as we had seen pull itself up on the wagon. So I stood there on sentry duty, my hand on the butt of my stunner, alert to any movement, until Illo was across. As a healer she wore no weapons—had refused the other stunner, and had only the long-bladed belt knife which was a working tool for any traveler. That would be useless against the scaled and armored thing.

Once she was across she turned a little and I was quick not to let her believe that I held back where she had led, setting foot on the first pile of stone to follow. Some of those stones, as I made the same jumps over the gaps, appeared unsteady and I wished I had had the foresight to bring with me the rope which had lashed the burdens on the gars. Linked so together, if one of us tumbled into the noisome appearing water the other could lend a hand.

As is mainly true when one fills the immediate

©AUSTIN-1980

future with imagined forebodings, we had no difficulty after all in winning into Voor's Grove. Directly ahead of where the bridge had once given access to what must have been the main street of the town that spotted unwholesome vegetation was thin. We slashed a path with our knives, to find that it had formed only a slight wall and we were now without a barrier.

"The flowers—!" I pointed to where those did indeed stand in place of the once familiar gardens which must have divided dwelling from dwelling.

As in Mungo's the brilliant blooms had looked almost like flames shooting from eternal but hidden fires. But—They were quiet. Quiet until we moved forward. I caught Illo's arm, held her so for an instant.

"Watch them!" I ordered.

They were still no longer. Instead they swayed, dipped, turned their wide expanse of gaudy petals this way and that. I had an unpleasant thought that somehow they were alive with a life we did not understand, and that their present movements were struggles to loosen the earth's grip upon their roots so that they could advance upon us.

"They sense us—" her voice was quiet, she did not attempt to move out of my hold. "That must be the truth—that they sense our presence."

At least none of them grew near the open passage which was the main road of the settlement. My thought that they could in any way move to attack us was childish folly. One cannot reasonably give such motive and desires to a plant—or at least I could not.

"What are they?" the girl was continuing. "Sentries —guards—?"

She made as if to move from the middle of the road,

closer to the nearest bed of those bowing, straining splotches of color. I held her back.

"I do not know what they are—but I feel we are better to remain at a distance."

"Perhaps you are right," she conceded.

156

Once again, as we approached the heart of the town, we could see that the ruin was not complete here. Houses stood sturdy enough though their once grey-white walls were stained green in places as if some mould or algae of sorts sought to defile them. For this vegetation was evil. I was as sure of that as I was of my own person. It was rotten, though that rot was not visible to the eye—it was the flowering of foul decay.

Suddenly Illo stopped short, her head swung about and she looked to a house on her right. It was no different from any of the rest we had passed—the same stained walls, the same mass of nodding, weaving flowers.

"What is it?"

"That—no—" she put her hand to her forehead. "For a moment, just a moment, I thought— Only I could not hold that thought. No, I can't remember!" Her voice arose a note or two, was a little desperate.

I suppose I should have suggested that we enter that dwelling, explore it. Perhaps it had been her home— But I could not possibly have forced myself, or allowed her, to cross into the territory of the flowers in order to reach the gap of the door.

We went on. Our pace was slow and I was sure that, even as I, she was listening, trying to make herself receptive to sound, sight, feeling—

The road brought us out, as in Mungo's Town, in the heart where stood the meeting hall. This one was different from that of the smaller town, for it had a series of booths erected to one side. I saw there piles of pottery, rotted streamers of cloth, the wares of merchants, now far gone in disintegration but making it clear that when the doom had come it had fallen on

157

a market day, or perhaps a fair when traders from down river had gathered here to bargain.

That expanse of gravel about the hall was empty—there was no line of skeletons. I drew a breath of relief. Perhaps, judging by the fact that my father had never reported such a find in his explorations and since the signs of certain death were missing here, Mungo's had been an exception to the general state of the deserted villages.

Illo left my side, walked purposefully toward the hall. "The place of records," she said as I hurried to join her.

For the first time I realized the important omission of my exploration of Mungo's. Of course—there was a small record room in each hall! Why had I not remembered that? I might only plead that the sight of the dead had driven it out of my mind. Also that I had been absorbed in the task which had sent me into the doomed village, the answer to the promise I had made. To leave my father's body with the other dead—that of his friends, his family—had been the purpose which had obsessed me.

The hall was the same as that I had seen, there was more ornamentation here as became the meeting place of a village which aspired to become a city. I saw painted on the walls the star symbols of four planets—those from which Grove people must have originally come. There was also a plaque which caught the eye because it was stark black and on it inserted in a glowing silver color, untarnished, was an inscription.

"To the memory of Horris Voor, opener of worlds, all honor.

May this, the last of his discoveries, prove his quiet resting place.

Earthed the rover, furled the star wings—
Peace comes at the end."

"Peace comes at the end," I repeated and a sound, which was not laughter but a cry to challenge all which must have happened here, followed my words.

Illo had gone to stand closer to the plaque, now she put a finger to trace some of those shining letters.

"He wanted life for his people; what did they gain here?" She shivered.

"Death," I concluded for her sourly. "He must have died before the doom came."

"I hope that he did," she returned. "I hope he died still believing that he had given a gift to the homeless. See those symbols," she gestured towards the inlays about the edge of the plaque. "You know those worlds, you must have heard of them. Would you care to live on any one of them?"

"*No!*" I did not know them of my own knowledge, I had never been crowded, imprisoned, hopeless, on a world where breeding had gone unchecked, or one which lived under iron dictatorship, or one where the need for the very bare necessities of life was so great that each day was a slavery of unending toil. Yes, the people from those worlds must have looked upon Voor as a kind of paradise. What kind of a hell had it really proved then to be?

"I wish—" she said very softly and I believed I knew her wish though she did not speak it aloud. From which of those worlds had her own kin come? Had she had a family—how big—brothers, sisters—?

At least they had known who I was when I had been found; I had had my father. But Illo had no one, and by her own account she had been at the mercy of those who had tried to stimulate her child's mind, to per- haps even shock her in order to answer questions. That she had survived and become the person she was, was perhaps as great an achievement as any of Horris Voor's when he had discovered a new world to open to the homeless, the restless, the oppressed.

"The records," her tone was decisive now as she turned her back firmly upon the wall.

As was true of every building I had seen from the outside, even the record room here had no door. I looked carefully at the wall. There was a series of small holes which had perhaps once held hinges. Doors and windows, gone—though the rest of the building or buildings about were intact, seemingly in good order. There were even those remnants of trade goods in the booths. Why—doors and windows?

Illo stood in the middle of the small side chamber. The walls held the racks for tapes, a number of them. Not only the records of the village would be here, but information tapes for learning. Or such should have been there. But every rack was empty. The reason occurred easily enough.

"Whoever came here, found you and the rest—they must have taken the tapes—"

"But then they would have been kept at Portcity. And those other doomed villages and holdings—there were no tapes from them on file either."

She had a point. If such tapes existed my father would certainly have used them. He had made his own records of the places he explored. However, though he went every time we visited Portcity to the record office, now I never remembered his asking for anything to do with the other sites prior to their abandonment. Missing tapes—who would want them and why?

In Mungo's the villagers had died. Had it been different in other places? That woman who had been found here in Voor with a broken mind—the one they had traced after her escape to the Tangle. Had she known something after all, something which the experts had not been able to get out of her with their probing in the short time before she had managed her flight?

"Who would want tapes?" I asked myself aloud.

"Some one— or thing—" Illo's mind made the same leap mine was making, "who wanted to know more about—us."

"This was an open planet," I objected to my own conclusion. "There was not even a trace of Forerunner artifacts ever found. Our detects registered no intelligence higher than that of the gars and maybe the mountain corands."

"What if there was a distort—" she said slowly. "The Tangle—it acts as a distort—we've learned that much."

Always the Tangle! I did not want to believe that the solution lay within that. No one would ever be able to penetrate it—not unless one of the huge hell-burst machines, which had long ago been outlawed for war on any Confederation or League world, could be found and brought here, its devouring fury unleashed on the grey blot. But then, if the Tangle *did* contain any intelligent life, enemy or not, we would never learn it. What a hell-burst was loosed against it consumed, until nothing was left but the bare rock bones of a planet and clouds of ashy dust.

"If our answer lies in the Tangle—" I shrugged.

"If it does—" but she did not sound defeated. When I stared at her, my attention drawn by something in her tone, I saw that she was gazing thoughtfully at those empty racks.

"There has to be intelligence!" There was a sudden new energy about her as if, having been shown a problem, she was now eager to be about its solution. "Have you ever been to the Tangle—to the very edge of it?"

"No. There was no reason—and—well, I don't even know of any loper who has. I've read the records at Portcity—they were enough."

"Not always. Most of those records were compiled by off-worlders."

"*Trained* off-worlders," I reminded her quickly.

"Yes, trained. But they are trained to depend on equipment. You have loper instinct—you must have. Could an off-worlder take out a trek wagon and travel without a guide, a gars-trained man?"

"He'd probably end by sending a distress call," I returned. All I knew of off-worlders were the miners and the ship people, and some merchants settled in Portcity. None of them could live off the plains, steer a course cross-country—or set a gar team on the trail. I used off-world equipment—but it was simple stuff—and I depended first on my senses more than any machine. In that she was right. Just as she might be able to heal a case some off-world medic would mark off as hopeless.

"So? Since the days when the settlements were first alive here there has been very little *our* people have tried to learn about the Tangle. The truth is—we have been afraid of it."

"With very good reason. Nobody lost in there was ever found—there were the two mapping flights from

Alsanban, they sent out their last reckoning over the eastern end of the Tangle. Then Hertzo's flyer and the Recki Company one—"

"Off-world—all of them."

"Lausur wasn't off-world," I pointed out. "His expedition made a sweep for forty days along the forepart back in 30 A.L."

"True. They made an edge sweep, but that was all it was—an edge sweep—"

"Sanzori!" I stared at her. "It was after Lausur that Sanzor was doomed!"

There might be nothing at all in the sequence of those two happenings, in fact no connection between them had occurred to me before, nor had I ever heard anyone speculate upon the fact that the doom of the first farthermost holding, a small one whose fate had then been ascribed to plague, had occurred just after Lausur's return from his long march, his tentative attempts to penetrate into the Tangle.

"If something was alarmed, made fearful—" Illo said slowly. "If to them—or—if we were as alien as that flood monster seemed to us—Lausur's march might have been taken as a threat, to meet with a counter."

"But it was two years before the next Shadow doom," I was trying now to remember my history. Luckily such facts had been well drilled into me.

"We might have been under observation—the fear or anger we aroused growing as we pushed farther north, closer to the Tangle. The first of the flyers crashed or was swallowed up during those two years— that was a Survey one. It would have had a great deal of equipment on board—"

What she said was making more and more sense, a kind of dark pattern. Threatened territorial rights was a very ancient cause for war. An animal—or a man—might fight before his own strip of country was invaded, or just at a suggestion that such an invasion threatened. And, supposedly if menaced by something wholly alien to himself, perhaps even in thought processes—fear would generate even higher to feed the anger.

"But why didn't some one figure that out—they've had plenty of time—years of it!" I near exploded.

"They were conditioned—conditioned to believe in reports, in the findings of machines—delicate and mainly accurate to be sure—but still machines, devised by men to help along our own process of thought, not perhaps wholly alien ones. Could such machines detect what their makers might not even be able to image exists?"

"The mine colonies have not been troubled. But they have the force fields. No village could afford to set up one, they would have no way of living inside. But if they strike at us—why not at Portcity—at the big places which are growing stronger—those south of the Halb? More settlers are coming in and settling in the south every season."

"It may just be," Illo was frowning a little, "that they cannot for some reason act at that distance—"

I noted that she now said "they" and not "it" or "something" as she had before. Our enemy was taking on a kind of nebulous shape which it had lacked. That this was all guesses was true, but at least it provided us with a starting point.

However I did not see yet how we could hope to

explore the Tangle—or why we should try. There are born into our species certain fears, rages, desires. These may be overlaid by the conditioning we receive during youth, still they can be awakened, and, once awakened, can drive us to action.

I had spent all I could remember of life trailing my father, who was, in turn, driven by an obsession concerning the Shadow doom. He had died because of an accident of nature, yes, but in his dying he had bound me to the same search, for the sight of the deaths in Mungo's had helped to shape me, too. Illo had come to the same path by more subtle means, but she would not, I knew, be turned aside.

What we could do at the Tangle I did not know; there was no solving its mystery. At least I could see none. Only piece by piece between us, we had built reasoning which would send us there.

Illo left the empty records room, came back into the open. I took a quick turn along that line of booths, peering at the remains of what had lain in each. There had been no attempt to cover over, put away, any of the wares. Improvised display counters had been fashioned of piled up transport boxes, and their tops were crowded with merchandise. Though time and weather had dealt hard with most of that.

I picked up a belt knife, to discover its length of tressteel, metal which could withstand years of constant use and exposure in the ordinary way, pitted, part of its length a lace of fine holes. A fast inspection of other metal wares showed that they all bore like signs. I clanged the knife down on the box on which it had lain. It shivered in my hand, splitting into small pieces. The hilt I tossed from me and then wiped my hand along the leather of my breeches at the thigh. That easy collapse of a metal which I well knew and had used all my life, trusting in its endurance, shook me badly. There had been that necklet which had lain for a long time in the grass and yet had shown not the slightest sign of wearing—except the brown links which had parted. Yet here the hardest of metal forging which I knew had not endured for even twenty years—far less—for Illo had come out of Voor Grove and she was younger than I. This fair must have been in progress on the very day the Shadow doom struck.

"You—the two babies—the woman—" I strode back to join her for she had not followed me but rather remained at the door of the hall, surveying the whole of the scene which she could sight carefully by a slow turn of the head, "were you all found together?"

"No." She shook her head. "It was a Voorloper who came. He was bringing an order from the port for—for —I cannot remember the name. But he saw what had happened, knew it when his wagon beasts refused to enter. I think he was a brave man for he came alone, knowing that sometimes the children were spared. He found the babies together in one house—I was trying to lead Krisan out, pulling at her hand. Only I was like one as witless as she then, crying, and babbling some strange words—He said later I was—singing—"

"Singing?"

"So he told it. He had to put restraints on Krisan for she would have run from him and she screamed terribly. I—I can remember that—only we were free of the town then. I was in the wagon wrapped in a blanket. Krisan lay on the floor of the wagon, rolling from side to side, trying to get free. First she screamed and I was very frightened—then she grew quiet all of a sudden and later she sang, sang and called—but her words were all strange and I was so afraid of her. The Voorloper headed across country to the mines and they took us out by flyer—only that night she chewed through the restraints—they had left her hands and feet roped because she was so wild. And she went— they trailed her to the Tangle—and reported her lost when they saw she had burrowed into that.

"The Tangle—it must be the Tangle!"

I showed her the broken knife and I saw her astonishment—"But that is tres-steel—" she exclaimed.

"And it breaks like rotten wood! Those devilish flowers—look at them!" A flutter of color had caught my sight. I whirled.

The flowers still moved a little, but not as they had. Only all their heads were pointed in our direction. Illo's suggestion that they could be watching us stood to the fore of my mind. How dared I deny that anything—even the least probable—could be true? I had lived on Voor all my life, been born here—but I was the alien—and there could be a thousand, a million secrets which my kind could not, dared not penetrate. If we were wise—

"The Tangle—" Illo said with the same resolution she had had when she insisted that a calling for need had brought her north.

"The Tangle—" I repeated heavily, knowing that there was no other way I could go—but this was indeed a road I might not have chosen but one I must follow to its end.

9.

We had traveled along the edge of the Tangle now for a full day, studying that massive barrier of intertwined vines, thorn edged bushes, thick branched, low growing vegetation. There were no flowers here— no sinister blooms which swung without air to stir them, petaled eyes to watch. Though the plants varied in shade, all were a darkish green-grey—near black and utterly unwholesome—at least to my eyes.

Oddly enough the gars had not held off as we drew near this alien stretch of country, as they had when we approached the Shadow doomed villages. Though they did not graze near the barrier, they seemed content to accompany us.

"Not a single break—" I pointed out in the later afternoon—

For some reason the Tangle appeared to radiate heat. I mopped my face with my arm, feeling as if I had been trudging miles under a midsummer sun, when I knew well that we were not far from the time of the frost bearing winds out of the north. What would those do to this mass of growth—or was it impervious to cold?

We had not attempted to touch it. Those finger-long spines on most of the outer rim bushes were enough to warn one off from such folly. If I packed a blaster instead of the tangler and stunner I might have experimented a little. But from all reports one could not even ray a way in. This whole expedition was folly and the sooner we admitted that the better.

Though one part of my mind kept assuring me over and over of that folly there was something else which kept me pacing doggedly on, scanning the Tangle. I had not the slightest idea of what we sought, yet I went. Illo, a little ahead of me, would stop every few steps and face the brush and vine wall, her expression that of one listening.

We camped that night a little away from the somber blot which seemed darker than any land ought to be. It was after we had eaten and drunk, crouching close to a very small fire fed from twists of dried grass which I fashioned out of my loper knowledge, that she said suddenly:

"The necklet—"

My hand was at my belt pouch—there was only one necklet. Now, in spite of a firm feeling that this was a dangerous thing, I brought it forth. Only to discover that it had another attribute, one which nearly made me drop it. We had found the chain under the sun, in the full light of day. Now dusk turned swiftly into dark, and in that dark the broken circlet glowed! I flinched. Yet the metal gave forth no heat, only that steady gleam of blue, enough to tint the fingers which held it.

"Give it to me!" Illo ordered.

"It—it may be a carrier—" I moistened my suddenly dry lips with tongue tip. There were alien metals said to radiate and that radiation reacting against a human body—acting upon human flesh—This had ridden against my body for hours—a couple of days. What could I have absorbed from it? For the skin of my pouch could not have shielded me from any radiation.

"It may be far more. Give it—!" Her voice was sharper, her fingers reaching to pluck the chain from my grasp.

"No!" I coiled my hand tightly around it. "If there is radiation—"

"Who could better judge such than a healer?" she asked.

She was right. Still, remembering how this find had affected her before, I did not want to yield it.

"What do you think that this has to do with the Tangle?" I hedged.

"Perhaps nothing, perhaps everything. It is old—it may go back to a beginning. It belonged to another people, perhaps *they* had a way, knowledge—Don't you see," her tone was near fierce now, "we must have a key, a guide—"

"To what? We have no way of knowing—"

"We must learn." She snatched then, her fingers pried at mine, and, rather than struggle with her, I had to allow her the chain.

She held the metal links closer to our pocket of fire. When the flame light touched the metal its own radiance dimmed. Illo slipped the chain back and forth, pulling at each link as if she wanted to test its strength, as a man tests a rope to which he is about to entrust his life.

"There is no radiation—as we know it," she reported. "There is energy, yes, but it is of another kind."

"What?" I wished mightily now that I had hurled that find from me back on the plains, sent it to be hidden once more under the thick growth of grass.

"Energy akin to an esper talent," she returned calmly. "You must know that when a sensitive uses such he radiates energy. That has been measured in a healer's work."

She spoke the truth, so much I could accept. However, that an inanimate object, such as this chain, could contain such energy—that was another matter. Illo still slid the links back and forth between her fingers. Then she laid across her palm the curved plate covered with intrate engraving which was as much a tangle of lines as the growth barrier we had been tramping by all day.

"Not yet." Slowly she opened the fingers she had curled around that plate. "But it will!" There was triumph in her voice, a light in her eyes which not just a reflection from the fire. "This—this *is* a key! Let me sleep with it and I shall know more." Once again her hand closed tightly over the coil of metal and I knew that she would not yield it to me. Still I was more than just uneasy to see that in her grasp.

A key—to what? I looked over my shoulder at the black blot which was the Tangle. The growth arose, a wall against all my kind. If this chain were a key to the opening of that wall—Only such a thought was folly.

She did not speak again, her mask was back in place, and she curled up at once on her grass bed. As

172

she settled her head I saw that the hand holding the chain rested against her cheek. It was wrong—the act meant danger—both thoughts were fast fixed in my mind. Only I dared not move to take that from her. I could have been somehow caught on the edge of her own concentration of her talent, which walled her off from any interference.

I walked away from the fire to where the gars grazed. Witol lifted his big head and whiffled at me, the snorting sound he made as a greeting. I drew my hand along his warm back where the patches of thicker winter hair were already growing, some near long enough to catch my finger tips.

Witol was part of the sane world I had always known. There was comfort in standing so beside the big animal, smelling the scent of his hide, feeling his hair under my hand. This was real. But picking at me eternally—since I had entered into Mungo's—sharper and sharper now, was an emotion which was part fear (I faced that squarely) and part something else, of which I was not yet sure—curiosity, a loper's desire to learn a new trail, a need for revenge on whatever had made this wide country a land of death for my kind? Perhaps a little of each.

I knew that I would go on in the morning, follow the useless path along the Tangle, hunting what never existed—a way in. Why—? This was like some tale from a story tape in which an impossible quest was laid upon some unfortunate and he was compelled by non-human pressure to continue to the end.

Voor's world. The planet had once seemed so open and welcoming—but perhaps my kind were never meant to—I shook my head vigorously as if I could so flip away that insidious conclusion. Each and every world which my species had colonized had had one problem or another. That quality of need for mastery, which was a birth-part of us, was always so awakened into life to set us hammering some very hostile planets into earth-homes. No world was ever a paradise without any danger. In fact such might have been far worse a pitfall for my kind than the worst stone-fire-airless hell. We would only have atrophied there—become nothing.

I scratched the upstanding tuft of coarse mane-hair between Witol's ears and he snorted happily, butted me with near strength enough to knock me from my feet. Our fire was like a fading eye—and weariness reached into me. Anyway our exploration would be limited by our supplies, as I had already made clear to Illo. We must turn south as soon as the water in the tanks Witol shouldered during the day reached a level I had scarred across the sides.

Back at the fire I added the last of my twisted faggots of grass, and then stretched out, my blanket over me. Though that curious warmth which had been with us all day still seemed to reach out even this far into the plains.

I shifted unhappily on my bed. Though I was tired enough to sleep, and to a loper strange places were no deterrent to rest—as long as they were in the open (for we of the trails find it difficult to rest easy within confining walls)—still my busy thoughts would not still. I turned upon my back and lay looking up at the stars. So had I seen those on many nights. Only then I had not been—alone—I had tried to keep from me that feeling which had struck, attempted to overcome me, at my father's death.

Now I fought that battle once again. From the time I had been small—the time I could remember at all—he had worked to prepare me for this kind of loneliness. There are many accidents and ills which whittle away at the numbers of lopers. A man may be asked for at Portcity, perhaps spoken of when one loper met another on the trail—but his fate never known. I had been taught as best my father could manage to be self reliant. If he had mourned my mother, others dead in Mungo's Town, he had never done so openly. As I have said he was not a follower of religious belief which was built upon a formal creed and ritual. Yet he had said at one or two rare moments that he believed the life essence we knew was but a part of something else which had an existence beyond our comprehension, and that we must accept death as a door opening and not a gate slammed shut.

Illo had had less than I during the years since Voor's Grove had been doomed. No one of *her* kin had remained to keep her in touch with normal life. I thought of what she had said about her ordeal when they had tried to make her remember. That she had made a place for herself with her talent testified to her courage and the stability of her mind.

So my thoughts wound back to what she was doing this night—sleeping with the touch of that ill-omened thing she had found. Suppose I moved now—tried to free the chain from her while she slept—or did she even sleep? Was she in some kind of trance? Should I —could I take it—?

I wanted to do just that, yet I found that such an act was impossible. Though I struggled against that unseen compulsion there was no chance for me to move. Slowly, though my thoughts still spun, I closed my eyes and slept.

There was the Tangle straight before me, and behind—or rather in me a compelling force sending me straight ahead at the fearsome thorny hedge which was its outermost defense—thorns to pierce the flesh viciously, blind the eyes. I threw up my hands to protect my face, fought to free myself. Still I strode on as if my path was as open and free as the plains.

I must be right against the thorns now, I had surely covered that small stretch of open ground. I dropped the hand I used to shield my face. There was before me light—a light which waxed and waned as might an earth-bound moon—save that it was not ruddy as Voor's moon might be. Then, as my eyes adjusted to that flickering light, I saw no moon disc; rather a pillar, as if some humanoid form had been set alight and was moving. Of the Tangle there was no sign—only that light which glided away, drawing me after it—

My heart beat heavily, I was gasping for breath as if I were running, and in me there was such expectancy, such a drawing that—

"Bart! Bart!"

Out of somewhere came a force to fasten on me, making me reel back and forth. Something held me back when I must go. That figure ahead was gaining ground—if I lost sight of it—

"Bart!"

I was pulled, lifted—I was awake!

Illo knelt beside me, both her hands were tight on my shoulders as if she had been dragging my weight up—or away—

"I—let me go—"

"Not that way!" She spoke crisply, nor did she loose her hold. She kept her link between us as if fearing I would lapse into some unconscious state again.

I blinked, shook my head.

"You are here," she said slowly, accenting each word, as she might if a child had wakened crying in the night. "You are here—and *now*—"

Though what she meant I did not understand. Gone indeed was that throbbing light. Behind Illo's head the sky was grey, lightning—the sky I had seen many times.

"I—I was—the Tangle—" My words twisted, as if, when I attempted to find those which best explained the vividness of that dream, I could not find the proper ones.

"Not *that* way," she repeated. "That is what *they* want—we go *our* way, not theirs."

She loosed her hold on me at last and I sat up. This was the camp we had made. There were the banners of a new day showing above the horizon. The fire was burnt out, still I felt no chill. On the other side of the pile of ashes the three gars stood, their large eyes watching me, seeming to hold a measure of that same studying look which Illo kept upon me.

"They? Who are *they*?" I demanded.

She did not gesture with her hands, rather she turned her head a fraction to point with her chin.

"I do not know—save that there is a form of intelligence somewhere in there—one I cannot tap. Which is aware of us—though—though it fears and so it weaves traps—not this time to catch bodies but minds. Here—"

She reached to her belt, holding out the chain. It was a complete circlet now, I saw that somehow she had bent together two of the broken links to make it whole.

"This you wear—"

I made no attempt to take it from her. "Why? I don't want—"

"Only you can use it. It is adapted to a male principle."

"Use it how?"

"I said it was a key—it is. One which that waiting there has reason to fear, or at least dreads. No," she silenced some of my unasked questions, "I received no more impressions than that. It must be worn by a man, and it will get us in—"

"Through that?" The thorned brush of my dreams was perfectly visible now. "We'd need a blaster—"

"I wonder." She sat back on her heels, her attention turned to the brush wall. "How does this vegetation react to a stunner?"

"React to a stunner? There could be no reaction to such a weapon. The power of that reaches into the nervous system, completely relaxes all muscles. It affects only animals and men. A plant has no—"

She arose, still facing the Tangle rather than looking to me. "We do not truly know what such a growth as this may have. That which attacked the doomed places is surely alien. What if this is even more so? Will it cost you anything to try?"

I had the two charges in the weapon, a dozen more looped in my belt. There was also a bag of them in the gear Wobru had been carrying. It would not be any great loss to prove to her that such a thing was impossible.

"I'll try," I promised. "You learned nothing more from that?"

The necklet was still in her hands. She glanced down at it and then thrust it vigorously in my direction. "Fleeting impressions—none I could fasten upon. The last thoughts of he who wore it were so chaotic I could not read them. Only that he had been sent on a mission when some evil struck, so that he could not fulfill his duty. That overrides much of the rest—his last despair at failure. But it has much to do with the Tangle, that is a matter I am certain of. Also he was on his way there when death took him—and only a man can pick from this what is needed."

The last thing I wanted to do was to take that necklet, fasten it about my throat. Perhaps it was because I so shrank from that act my pride was aroused. Illo was used to dealing with things of her talent—the "unseen." She could accept this all as something which one must do, even as a Voorloper would inspan his wagon before he drew out from a camp. To her my squeamishness might seem without any base except craven fear of the unknown.

Well, I admitted to myself, that I did have. Still there was enough determination left in me so I must prove to myself, if not to her who might not understand, that I was not to be defeated by the unknown before I put up a struggle. Realizing that I must do this quickly, without stopping to consider what might happen, I caught the necklet from her, worried open the clasp and set it about my neck, making tight the fastening once again.

It fitted so well, lying just at the base of my throat,

that it might have been fashioned for me. The collar of my hunting shirt was loose, since in this strange warmth I had not tightened the lacing thongs. So there was nothing between the smooth metal and my flesh. That inscribed foreplate lay directly in front.

A sudden thought crossed my mind—on some planets there were animals trained to serve men, animals with not the same grade of intelligence as the gars, or ones not so amiable. Those creatures bore the seal of their ownership—collars—some patterned with the name of the owner. Suppose—suppose this was such a collar and I had so voluntarily accepted subserviance to a will I did not know and perhaps could not even understand? But I did not mention this to Illo.

She reached up when the necklet was in place and touched, with only fingertip, that plate at the base of my throat. The metal was not cool against my skin, instead it seemed to have the same temperature as my body.

"Duty—" she said the one word slowly, as if meditating on what it meant. "He was in such anguish of mind because of his duty—he tried to fight off death because he had not fulfilled what he must do."

"Could you tell who he was—or," I hesitated and then added, *"what?"*

She considered that question for what seemed to be a long moment.

"He was humanoid—I think—At least this fits you so well it might have been made for you. But his mind —it was different. Only his emotions were plain to read—that because they so rent him at the end. It all happened very long ago." She made a queer little gesture with both hands as if scattering something on

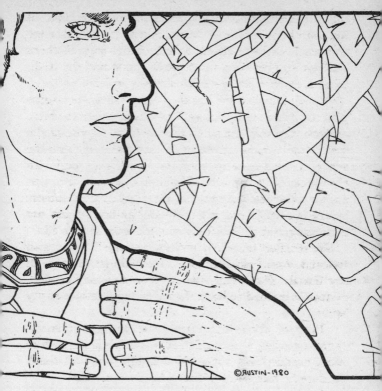

©AUSTIN-1980

the ground—perhaps fragments of all those lost years which had clung to the necklet until she decided it must be used.

We broke camp, loading the gars. Instead of ranging ahead today, the three beasts fell into single line behind us. They could have been in yoke to a small wagon. Nor did they break that line to graze. Illo, for I left the guide point to her, did not advance directly toward the portion of Tangle by our camp. Rather she set out again on a parallel route westward.

We had been tramping so for some time and the sun was already well up, when she halted abruptly, faced the Tangle wall. To my eyes this portion differed in no way from that we had surveyed along the way we had come. Yet she stared straight at the thorned brush and ordered:

"Try the stunner—here!" She stretched out one arm, her index finger pointing at a bush which overtopped my own head by a good half length of my body.

I drew my weapon, feeling slightly foolish, for I believed that its charge would only be wasted. However, I must use it, if for no other reason than to prove that fact to my own satisfaction as well as to her.

My pressure on the firing button was steady; I had set the power to top force. Now I swung the barrel of my weapon slightly, playing the invisible ray up and down the bush she had indicated. Nothing—just as I had thought. However, as I let the stunner slide back into its holster, she was running toward the bush.

"Thorns—!" I warned her.

She had already put out her hands, though I noted she did catch only the tips of the branches where their armament was the least. Then—

Had I not seen it I would not have believed that it might happen. Illo had given a jerk. The brush moved forward a little in answer to her tug, then wilted. That was the only word I could use to describe its sloughing downward, the seemingly instantaneous withering of leaf, the limpness of branch. There was a gap in the wall!

"Again!" She shouted that at me, her face flushed, her eyes alight. No mask on her now, she was all aroused eagerness. "Again!"

So I followed her orders; an inner bush withered, taking with it to the ground a huge matted mass of vine. We had the beginning of a path. However, the outer portion of the Tangle had yielded in the past to something far more potent than any stunner—blaster fire—only to regenerate, rising from the roots thicker, more deadly than before.

I reached the edge of the gap, threw out my arm and caught her, dragging her back.

"Wait—it may grow again!"

Her face showed a flash of anger, but she did not try to pass me. I had no idea how long it had been before the regeneration on those earlier expeditions. Still certainly it could not have been too long or the process would not have so impressed the would-be past explorers.

We waited. There was no change in the withered growth. I was as suspicious as I might have been with a stunned sand hound. For I could not shake off the feeling that perhaps this was a game—if you will— being played by something that was well prepared to defend itself and had successfully done so for generations.

No sign of life came, no movement of branch or even straightening of crumpled leaf. Illo turned on me:

"Would you wait away the day?" she demanded.

I wanted to say "yes, if need be." Yet I did not. As far as I knew from past records, and my father had indeed combed those, playing the tapes over and over again, the stunner had never even been considered as a weapon of possible use against the Tangle. Why should it have been? It could be that so simple a discovery would have made the expeditions free of its secrets long ago.

I checked the charge in my weapon carefully. About a quarter of it had been expended—and I did not know how far we might go—or what else could lie before us. Voorlopers are a mixture of the daring and the wary— that is, they must be if they continue to live. One part of me wanted to push forward, the other was uneasy— this answer was *too* simple.

"We must go!" Illo twisted away from me, started forward, planting her boots firmly on the first layer of wilted vegetation. I roused from my indecision and hurried on, elbowing by her, to once more spray the growth, watch it wither, grow limp, and sink to form a carpet. There was a snort from behind. I looked around and saw, to my true amazement, that Witol was coming too, his herd mates behind him.

Now I was aware of something else, as I stood and sprayed to open the way. There was a rustling through the Tangle, though I could not, in the pocket the stunner had opened, feel any breeze. I moved with the utmost caution, looking from side to side. The nodding flowers which had studded the villages of the dead were in my mind. Those had moved without any wind's help also. Was it the leaves, the branches, those strangling vines, which set up that sound here?

Nothing encroached on the path the stunner opened. In fact, I thought, though I could not be sure, that the growth seemed to edge back. If it had not before come in direct contact with the ray I wielded, it now had enough sensation, or intelligence of a sort, to fear contact. Surely the path *was* wider than the space I had rayed, wide enough so Illo and I advanced abreast and

the gars had no trouble in single-filing behind us, not even their burdens of gear scraping so much as a leaf on either side.

We advanced slowly, for after each spraying I determined to wait a space to be sure there was no swift renewal of life. I had to refit the stunner twice with fresh units. When I looked back it was down a long tunnel, the other end of which had near disappeared. We could not keep on so forever. Either we must find some natural clearing in this nightmare of an alien wood, or carve us one in which to rest.

That dank heat which had reached us even as we had only skirted the edge of the Tangle was far more oppressive here. Sweat ran down my face, lay under my shoulder pack to fret my shoulders. The half-healed scratches from the fight when I strove to get us and our gear out of the wagon stung furiously. Luckily there was not what I feared we might find here—no noxious insects swarmed about us to sting or bite.

Our progress became a set pattern: ray, wait, advance, ray, wait, advance—

Until—

A mass of the Tangle fell in the usual way to the ground, that ground which gave off a sour smell of its own. The disappearance of the growth left something standing—something which no stunner could possibly affect—a pillar of black stone—and it was no natural spur of rock either.

10.

Nor was it a pillar we faced. For, as the last of the foliage melted away, I heard Illo's breath go out in a hiss and I was startled into raising my weapon to give another blast which was not needed. What stood in our path, slightly larger than life size, was a statue carved of dull black stone, but with such fidelity to detail it might have been a living creature frozen by some means to act as a guard against further intrusion.

It was humanoid in contour though there were differences. The hands which had been raised to cross on the breast had six fingers, the face was more markedly oval than any Terra-human's, while the nose extended well out, having a definite hook of the broad tip. There was no sign of any representation of hair save on the very top of the head where there stood erect a crest looking not unlike flaps of skin a lizard might own.

Though the whole of the body was done in exacting detail, there were no eyes represented in that face, only dark pits where such should have been. Also there were no sexual characteristics such as were common to my own kind. It could have been masculine, feminine,

or neither. But that it had been fashioned to represent in mirror-exact fashion a living or once living creature I had not the least doubt.

As I continued to study the face, that impression of menace which had been born in my mind from its sudden appearance and its being set in that alien form faded. I felt instead a brooding sadness, as if it had been placed as a memorial, rather than intended to warn off those who managed to enter the Tangle this far.

The stone of which it had been carved had no counterpart in any I had seen on Voor. The entwined mass of vegetation, the passing of what must be an untold number of seasons, had done nothing to dull or erode the work. It stood now uncovered, as clear in all its lines as if it had been only recently set in place by the artist who had conceived it. It was not beautiful by our standards, no, but still it had a power—a purpose—for it conveyed stronger and stronger that hopeless feeling of what I now believed to be defeat, resignation to extinction.

"They knew " Illo's voice was hardly above a whisper.

I understood her meaning. Yes, whoever had wrought this monument had known that there would be no future—no way to go except to an ending. The more I looked upon it the more my own spirit sank, the greater appeared our folly in trying to penetrate a wilderness of the alien which was never meant to be invaded by our kind.

"No!" Illo caught at my arm. "Do not let it do that to you! Do not let it make you think–feel failure!"

She could not have read my emotions, she must have

judged them entirely by her own reaction to that sombre, brooding monument to despair. Perhaps that was its weapon! Perhaps it formed a trap, not for our bodies, or even our minds, but our spirits. Still it took almost all the determination I could summon to walk forward, approach that silent statue.

More and more it did not appear to be a work of art, rather something which had once lived and now had been left, unable to completely die. I found myself staring mainly, as I advanced, at those pits in which eyes should have rested, half fearing, half believing, that I might see there sparks of life, even if such had withdrawn from all the rest of the frozen body.

The dead black color—had that been selected because the creature itself had been that color in life? For that it represented a living species, even a living or once living person, I no longer doubted. I found myself passing to the right while Illo broke her grasp on me and went to the left, the statue for an instant between us.

Heat—a surge of warmth reached me from that stone. I had no wish to put out a hand and touch it— I could not have forced myself to make such an investigation. Only the black figure might have been a torch radiating heat outward.

I heard the grunting of the gars. They had come to a stop. I swung around, to blast with the stunner the growth on one side, giving them greater room to pass the figure by. They seemed reluctant to move on for the first time since they had so followed us into the Tangle. Witol raised his head and bellowed, as he might when delivering a challenge to some audacious bull intruding on what he considered his own territory.

Would the animals turn back? I felt that no urging of mine would influence them, that now they moved by their own volition and could not be controlled by my commands. So I waited.

Witol challenged for the second time. There was something in the massed walls about the small space the stunner had cleared which gave back, in odd, hollow echoes, his cry. Reluctantly the bull lowered his head and paced on, his two companions falling in single file behind. I saw him swing his head to one side so that even the tip of his horn might not touch the figure. However, he had chosen—and in our favor. Once more I began my task of raying open a way before us. Still the vegetation answered with withering, crumbling of limb, curling of leaf.

"Forerunner—surely—" Illo kept her voice low. She might have feared some listener. "Have you heard of or seen its like before?"

I tried to remember the tapes which my father had collected and poured over. There had been many Forerunner civilizations; men realized that as they spread outward to take over planets which had once been colonies, or the homes of unknown races now vanished. There were worlds which were nothing but one huge, deserted city, the tall buildings based on every inch of available land—their original populations too great for us to fathom—all emptied by time. There were worlds which had been burnt off, turned into radioactive cinders, or half devastated, with glassy craters where cities or points of military installation had stood.

Wars which had been perhaps galactic-wide in that remote past had swept away races, species. It must have happened over and over again—civilizations which built, reached for the stars, grew powerful, established federations or empires, then fell apart in wars, in plagues, in slow decay when stellar commerce failed and no star ships came.

My own species was very young compared to stellar time. Though we were spreading fast, building, trying to wrest from the reminders of the past we found more and more of their secrets. There were many Forerunners, yes, and at different times, on different worlds, or in different sectors.

The Zacathans with their great storage banks of historical knowledge might have a clue to that figure, but if so it was on a tape my father had never found. Only, and now a new excitement came to life in me, a Forerunner find—a big one—that would mean complete freedom for both Illo and me. For the finder's fee for such was untold credits. We could go anywhere, do whatever we willed—if this was Forerunner.

"They faced certain death—" Illo's thoughts had not swung so wide or in such a selfish direction as mine. "They had and expected no hope—"

I had tried not to think what that mourning figure had meant—its defeat was too plain, enough to dishearten us.

"In their time," I commented. "Their time is past."

She did not answer me at once. I think she was still caught up by the emotion that lost statue had engendered. Perhaps because she was a healer, trained to be attuned to the ills of others, it had struck far more deeply with her than with me. For a loper learns early that good and ill both exist, and sometimes the ill outweighs the good, but both must be accepted and dealt with to the best of one's ability.

As the stunner cleared our path I half expected to uncover more such relics of the unknown. But we were well beyond that statue, which was either a warning or the monument to the death of a people, before the growths melted away to disclose now the beginnings of walls. What we had come upon by chance was a gateway, one which lacked any sign of door or barrier, while the walls stretched away on either side to be swallowed up quickly by the Tangle. There was an arch overhead, a shallow one with only a slight upward curve.

Illo once more caught at my arm. "Look!" Her other hand swept up toward that arch. That had been fashioned of the same dead black stone—as were the walls—but it was not smooth. Instead it was carved in a twisted, intricate design, one in which you could distinguish nothing but curves and lines which led nowhere. Save that the longer you studied them the more the idea grew upon you that this was no abstract adornment but had a meaning. Perhaps it was an inscription in a language which expressed its symbols in a way totally alien to those we could ever understand.

"The necklet!" My companion reached up to catch the edge of my skin shirt, dragging that down and away from the ornament I had so reluctantly put on that morning.

"There is a sameness—" she declared.

I fumbled one-handedly, the stunner still at ready in the other, trying to loose the clasp so that I might compare. Only that fastening would not yield.

"Unfasten it—" I ordered Illo.

She slipped the chain about, as I bent my head and stooped a little, so that she might be able to more

speedily find the clasp.

"It—it is gone!"

"No it isn't—I can feel it—" I objected.

"Not the necklet—the fastening!"

"What!" I rammed the stunner into her nearest hand and began feeling along the chain for that clasp. There were no slightly larger links—nor did I feel the place where she had mended the chain so that it could be worn—that place where she had squeezed two of the broken links together. It was as smooth as if it had been sealed on me.

I caught my fingers in it then and strove to tear it off. All that happened was that the links cut into my neck with knife-edge sharpness and I had to stop.

"You can't see the clasp, or the mended place?" I demanded.

I could feel the chain once more slipping about, this time in her touch.

"Neither is there! But I don't understand—"

What I understood was an impossibility. There was no way for the clasp and the repaired breakage to so meld into the chain as to be now undetectable. Yet I could not believe that she was deceiving me, and certainly my own fingers had not been able to locate any irregularity in the necklet either.

"Perhaps it was made to respond so—to body heat or the like," Illo said slowly. "I have heard of the Koris stones—is it not true that they only come alive and take on their jewel brightness and fragrance when worn against bare skin? Might there not be an unknown alloy of metal which fastens of itself under the same conditions?"

True or not, I was unhappy that the alloy had answered so to *me*. I had not been easy when she had first suggested my wearing the chain. I was really disturbed now.

"Take my belt knife and see if you can cut through it," I ordered.

She drew back from me and her answer was blunt and instant.

"No!"

"No? Why? Do you think I am going to keep wearing something I can't rid of—"

"Which you must *not* get rid of."

Her voice held such authority that I simply stared at her in open disbelief.

Since I could not very well use the knife myself, I was to go collared to her pleasure. My resentment, fed by fear as I will freely admit, then flared.

"Explain to me why—" I strove to keep my voice even, not to let explode the anger building in me.

"I cannot. I only know that in some way, which we shall learn, you must bear this—"

My teeth snapped together, I would not allow her to guess my fear. Instead I thumbed on the ray of the stunner which I snatched back from her, spraying ruthlessly and recklessly ahead at what lay beyond the arch, clearing a way for us within the only partly visible walls.

The ray diminished with my continued attack, until I realized that, in my rising fury, I had exhausted the current charge. That sobered me. For we had no idea how far this mass extended, nor how much longer we would have to call upon the stunner for service.

I snapped in a new unit, but did not look at or speak to her. With every breath I drew I was aware of that chain making me, as I believed, a slave to some force which was the worse because I did not know what it was or in what way it would next show that it was master.

There was a nudge against my shoulder, imperative, delivered with a force which nearly sent me sprawling forward to land face down in the wrack of the plants I had mown down. Witol's mighty bellow, the loudest I had ever heard from his thick throat, echoed about our ears. He edged by me, his burden of the water tanks on which we depended scraping, pushing me, sending me against Illo.

Head down, the bull pawed the ground, sending bits of wilting leaves, slimy under soil, flying behind him. His eyes glinted redly and he was the picture of growing rage, as if he had caught fire from the same emotion which had earlier possessed me.

Bru echoed his bellow with her higher call, striving to draw even with her mate. While Wobru momentarily arose on his hind legs as if longing to lunge forward, but found no way he could make room for himself beyond the broad backs of the two older gars.

What had so aroused Witol and the others I could neither see nor guess. To my closest survey the unsheared brush ahead still presented exactly the same appearance as it had all along. Nor, when the echoes of the gars' cries died away, was there anything to be heard. Only Witol and his mate had passed under that archway and there was nothing left for us to do but follow.

Without realizing until after I had made the gesture, my hand went again to the chain about my throat as I passed under that arch. What warning or greeting did that fanciful involved script hold? What relation might such have to the badge I wore now in spite of myself?

The gars had paused, Witol's nose near touching the bank of Tangle which had not yet yielded to the stunner. I worked my way around the side of the gar, trying to avoid touching any unwithered stuff, any thorns. Once more I sprayed ahead, widening the ray to the farthest extent the weapon would allow, then, in turn, swinging it back and forth to make a broader path.

So on we went, nor did there appear as yet anything else which that growth concealed. If the wall was guarding a village, or even the buildings of a holding—then where did such stand? The vegetation fell to reveal nothing but a mass of the same beyond.

Witol halted so suddenly that I bumped against his massive shoulder. He did not yield and now I could not push past. His head swung low, and one of his horns caught in the matted stuff which lay dead or dying on the ground. He tossed and the vegetation flew, he pawed and earth glistening with slime appeared. Only that broke also as he deliberately dug one horn down into it, tossed, pawed. Great chunks of tainted soil flew out and away. There arose so putrid and foul a smell from his efforts that I gasped. Illo held one hand to close off her nose.

There was something—under that coating of diseased soil (for all I could think of was that the very earth itself here bore no relation to the clean dirt of the plains). Witol's efforts uncovered a smooth surface, one which was still streaked, it was true, with greasy, evil smelling clay—but one which certainly was not normal ground.

Witol worked industriously, first with one large cloven hoof, and then the other. Wobru shouldered aside his mother and came behind the greater bull, beginning in turn to paw at earth his sire had already disturbed. While Illo and I watched with amazement, the gars, laboring together as if they were teamed, cleared a space which was growing larger by the instant. Now and then Witol turned his head to me to grunt. His meaning was so plain that I, who had always commanded the beasts, now obeyed his orders, sweeping the stunner—killing and then stepping aside to let the gars clear away the debris.

We were no longer in a tunnel of vegetation. Rather we stood in a clearing which was roughly square, swept nearly clean through the efforts of the animals, floored with a metal which I judged to be the same as that of the necklet I wore.

Though the poisonous and foul growths of the Tangle had covered it perhaps for eons of time, the surface showed no sign of rust or erosion. What might be its purpose and what had led the gars to act as they did were both mysteries I did not attempt to solve. Illo stooped but did not quite touch that flooring.

"It is not pavement, I believe—" she studied the expanse carefully. To my eyes there was not a single sign of any break in it—the whole piece was a giant plate.

The gars had finished their cleanup and now stood quiet, the heads of all three hanging low, their noses near touching the plate. Were they in search of a scent? Were they looking for something? I had passed the point of amazement now; I was not sure of anything. Before my eyes the beasts I had always taken for

animals, of some intelligence, but still animals, had
engaged in action which suggested that all our esti-
mates concerning them were very wrong, that they
were far more than prize stock to serve settlers on
Voor. It was at that moment I began also to wonder
whether they were not, as a species, far older and longer evolved than we had ever guessed. Had their long-
ago ancestors indeed known the race who had set this
plate they now revealed to us?

Illo cried out, stumbling a step or two towards me.
I met her and we clung together. That platform which
had appeared so intact, so solid, was sinking, and we
were being carried downward with it.

I tried to reach the edge, drawing the girl with me.
Witol took a ponderous step or two, setting his large
body broadside to cut me off from any escape. Before
I could push around him we were already too deep, so
that even a leap would not have allowed me to catch
the edge of the break.

The gars stirred and I heard Wobru grunt uneasily.
I say heard, for, as we sank, there was a darkness closing in about us. That patch of light was still above us
—now far above us. Our rate of descent seemed to be
more swift than we were aware of—otherwise no light
appeared to pierce into the depths into which the platform carried us.

Illo held onto my hand with a grip so tight that her
nails cut into my skin, but I made no move to loosen it.
Just now it was good to have that touch, to reassure
myself that I was not insane or hallucinating, that this
was really happening.

I now had to turn my head well up, back on my
shoulders, to watch that fast disappearing square of

sky which I could not hope to reach. While all about us was a darkness which was heavier and more solid than any moonless night could be. There were no stars here to reassure us with their light.

"Bart!" Illo had turned a little in my hold. I looked down and saw her face. There was a curious blueish light across it. "The necklet—it is afire!"

Afire! I felt no more heat than that subtle warmth which I had been aware of since I first put the chain on. The circlet fit so tightly to my throat that I could not see it, but I could catch a radiance which appeared to stream out across my breast and shoulders.

I loosed my other hand, temporarily thrusting the stunner back into my holster, and in turn worked free the torch from its thongs at my belt. My fingers found the "high" button and a moment later the ray swept out and around.

We were descending into a well, the walls of which were coated by the same alloy as formed the platform on which we stood. That fitted exactly to the walls, sliding down them with no sign of any space between. There were no visible openings, not a seam to be detected along those walls—as if the whole tube had been cast as a single great piece. Nor was there any chance of a hand or foothold on that smooth surface. Unless the trap which was this platform could be controlled in some manner, we were perhaps to be buried alive in an installation which was a total mystery.

I looked to the gars. They stood as quietly as if they were waiting in sedate sequence as they always did to be inspanned before a move-out. Why—and what—and who—?

I did not voice such question. Illo knew no more

than did I, and I could expect no answer from Witol. However I kept the torch sweeping about the walls, seeking some opening, some hope of escape. Still we continued to drop smoothly down.

The open patch at the top was now smaller than my hand; I could not even estimate how far beneath the surface we had come. There flashed into my mind scattered bits of the information my father had culled from the Forerunner archives. There had been apparently some races or species among them who had had a liking for undersurface life, building strange and unknowable installations in caves, in burrows they tunneled, as if they were more at home in such places than on the surface of the worlds they chose to visit—or to colonize.

Perhaps this race, if it were not native to Voor (though a vanished native civilization could not be ruled out) had been of that type. There must come an end to our journey soon. This, I had come to believe, was not a trap for prisoners (or at least I hoped that was so), rather an entrance to some place of importance.

The end did come—as the platform suddenly passed the tip of an opening in one wall, pulled on, down and down, until there was a wide door open before us. Then it came to an abrupt halt.

I half expected the gars to take the lead in disembarking, I do not know why. However, the beasts showed signs of uneasiness, snuffling and moving their feet as if they were not quite sure of the stability of the platform, though it no longer moved.

There was nothing to do but to go on, through that doorway which seemed a cup of pure dark, hoping that somewhere beyond there might just lie some means of returning to the surface. I said as much and Illo agreed.

Now that we had reached the bottom of the well, she appeared to have regained her confidence—or at least put on the appearance of doing so. I had to admit to myself that action as represented by the waiting doorway renewed my spirits also. Shoulder to shoulder we stepped from the platform into the waiting corridor or tunnel. Once more the gars fell in behind us as they had when we had broken our path into the Tangle.

I swept the torch from side to side. This appeared much like the shaft we had descended—or its lesser twin—being laid upon its side. The same smooth, seamless walls, no breaching of those, no sign of another doorway, of any exit except the one we followed.

"Switch off the torch a moment," Illo said.

I did not know what she wished to learn, only I did as she bade. Then we discovered that the light I carried was no longer necessary. Though perhaps not as bright as the radiance from the necklet, there was a dim glow to which our eyes adjusted, enough so that we could walk without difficulty seeing ahead. I was glad to save the torch and fastened it back in my belt, taking once more the stunner. Not because I expected to encounter any more of the Tangle's foul mass but because with it in my hand I found a certain reassurance, an illusion perhaps that I might still be in some control of the situation were we to discover— what? Some alien form of life—some mechanical installation—which had been left to run through endless time by its vanished creators? I did not know, nor did I try to speculate, I only knew I felt safer with the stunner in my fist.

The road seemed endless. So much so that once we stopped, drank from our supply of water, sharing that in small measurement with the gars, eating our trail bread. I gave a cake of this to each of the beasts and they chewed noisily, apparently finding it to their taste. At the back of my mind stirred the thought that once our supplies were gone—No—that would I face when the time came. We would be as prudent with both food and water as we could, and I would not say aloud what might be the end of such blind wandering.

At the end of the corridor was a door. This was closed, though I could see the slit which marked it clearly when I once more loosed the torch and had Illo hold it that I might examine the barrier. There was a cup-like pocket to my left but no latch that I could distinguish. I fitted my fingers into that depression and strove to push, but the barricade remained immovable. Was it locked and we prisoners?

There was one other thing to try. Once more I braced myself and used fingers as best I could, this time pushing towards my right instead of inward. For a long moment I thought that my guess was a failure. Then, perhaps as the result of centuries of disuse was overcome, it did slide reluctantly, taking all my strength to force it along. I discovered that a series of sharp jerks were better to stir it a little at a time, accomplishing more in that way than any steady pull. The panel was open at last, and with its opening light spilled through—a light which was almost as bright as day in the upper, outer world.

11.

Light streamed from above, steady and clear, while between us and its source reached a flight of broad, shallow steps. The surface of each step was inlaid with color, brilliant color. The designs were—faces!

There was nothing inhuman or alien about these representations as there had been in the face of the statue guardian we had passed in the Tangle. These were of people who might have lived in any holding or village. While each varied from the next, possessing such life-like features I could only believe that they had been originally fashioned to resemble once living personalities, still they had been carefully set so that anyone climbing the stair, no matter where he would put his feet as he went, would tread upon one or another of them.

There was something unpleasant in their cast of countenance, a slight exaggeration of this feature or that, the beginning of a sly smirk, a leer of the eyes. On close examination one could well believe that whoever had wrought this stairway had done it in a mood of hatred and vengeance. To tread upon the helpless face of the enemy—that was a conception which in itself was a token of so strong a fury that it shook one.

Illo went down on her knees, put out her hands to touch the nearest of the faces on the bottom step. It was as if her finger had fallen on a coal of living fire, so did she instantly jerk away.

"They—there are skulls—or a skull here, Bart—under the pattern face, a real skull."

As I knelt beside her I could see nothing but the surface. It must have been her fine-tuned healer's touch which had read the horror beneath the covering.

"Their enemies—how great was their rage—!"

"These could not be our people." My mind pictured instantly for me those lines of skeletons at Fors. Those bones had been intact, the skulls all there. This place was old, it had existed, I was certain, long before the coming of the First-In Scout of our kind to discover Voor.

"No—much older. But like us." She looked up at the doorway above, from which that light streamed. "We must go on—but to walk so—" she shivered.

I studied the faces carefully. Yes, they were all unlike, all realistic representations. But still human—as human seeming as I was.

"This happened a long time ago," I assured her. Though what "this" might have been I could not understand, save that the stairway might have been erected to celebrate a final victory, a crushing defeat—for who—the builder, or those they had pictured? Had one race or species been driven from the surface of Voor, taken precautions to exist here, then wreaked its vengeance on visitors in such a monstrous form? Or was the answer just the opposite: the aliens had won and celebrated their victory with an everlasting portrayal of the conquered? In any event the artist who had designed this had shown with merciless accuracy all the meanness, cruelties and evils my species was capable of in those subtle lines on the faces.

"Long ago—" she echoed. "But they tried—to seal them in—their enemies. The skulls—it is evil! Evil!"

I stood up, and, when she did not move, I stopped and drew her to her feet.

"There is nothing to be done now. I do not believe that more than bone was sealed here—"

"We do not know." She turned her head a little so her eyes met mine. There was a deep horror in them. Plainly she was shaken as I had seldom seen her. "How can we understand what happened here once? A tomb is a quiet place in which nothing any longer sleeps—it is but a place of memories for the living, and, as years pass, ceases to be even that. Such a thing as this keeps old hates terribly alive." She shivered. "We do not know what they believed—and belief is a very potent weapon—as well as a guard—"

"*We* do not believe!" I thought I knew what she hinted at and it shook me for a moment, but only for a moment. Such a suggestion was something I refused to accept. If one did not believe then this threat had no existence.

"Yes—" Her voice was still shaken. She no longer looked at me, her eyes turned once more upon the steps, though her hand lay on my arm and she did not draw away from me.

"Peace—peace be unto you! To those who wrought and those who died in the making—peace! For all is gone—and now forgotten. Rest you both in a final and unending sleep of peace."

It did not seem strange that she would speak so. I had none of her talent, still I had been disturbed when I looked upon the paintings made to be trod upon many times over. Now I did not look at them; I would not allow myself to gaze from face to face.

Close together, her hand remaining on my arm, we climbed that stairway. I heard the hooves of the gars clinking on the stones as they came after. Nor did we look down again at what we trod upon. Perhaps Illo was trying as hard as I was to force from her mind, as we went, the possible meanings of that staircase.

The quality of that light ahead impressed me. It was a very long staircase, with rises so shallow, steps so wide, I began to wonder if we were not indeed once more approaching the outside world and if what beckoned us on was not true daylight. However, as we reached the head of the stairs, and looked ahead through a very wide portal, we did not see the open land, neither the plains nor the rank growth of the Tangle.

Illo's startled cry of wonder matched my own exclamation of amazement. We might be stepping into one of those experimental stations such as I had seen on tapes, where plant life studies were in progress. Raised sections of the same alloy stood in straight rows. Each formed a trough or bin filled with soil. Some gave rooting only to dried stalks and skeletons of plants, others were rankly luxurious with still living growth.

Overhead floated a cloudy, misty covering which drifted in patches, as if indeed miniature clouds had been imprisoned here. Those moved, slowly, though

now and then one paused over one or another of the bins to loose a shower of moisture.

Above those drifting cloudlets spread a criss-cross network of what looked to be bars. Some of these held a core of light. Others were dark in random patches. The light which some did supply was not unlike the sunlight of the outer world, just as the warm humidity of the place was that of a mid-day in the south at the season of sowing.

Still there was nothing resembling a conventional garden in this display. Those plants nearest to us which were alive were strange to me. As we advanced farther into what must be a very large chamber, for we could not see the other end, we passed close to that first planting of living vegetation.

I cried out, jerking Illo away just in time. Out of what had looked not unlike a clump of ferns had arisen a whip-lash of tendril, moving also with a whip's agility, to fall just short of where the girl had stood a moment earlier.

The tendril-vine (or whatever it might be) struck out again, while the fern-part from which it came rocked and swayed, as if so eager to seize upon any intruder that it was attempting now to move its roots to reach us. We skirted that warily, brushed against the side of another planting place which held only the dead, while the tendril continually flailed after us.

"Keep away from the planted boxes." My order was unnecessary after that display. Illo would have lingered to watch the continued struggles of the thing, but I pulled at her again. The sooner we reached the other end of this place (if it had an end at all) the better. I was, however, careful to steer a zigzag path, passing beside the beds where there was nothing living. I thought of leading the gars. Though whether the tendril could have held one of the large beasts to any purpose I did not know. It could, of course, have some other method of subduing its prey—say poisoned thorns—as far as I knew. When I looked back I saw that Witol and the rest, pacing again in a straight line, were following our own maneuvers, and my inward questioning about the intelligence of the animals once more arose.

We were at the side of the fifth of the planted boxes away from the entrance when I came to sudden halt. For what faced us were the same flowers which had appeared to watch us in the Shadow doomed villages. Their colors were not as strident here, and they were smaller. But that they were of the same species there was no question. Also, as we neared their position, they had deliberately turned their heads to face us, and that bowing, weaving which was caused by no wind began.

For some reason here they seemed even more sinister than those others had in the open—perhaps because this was their own place (how long ago had they been planted and by whom?) where in the destroyed settlements they had been left unchecked or culled. Their unusually fleshy stems made a slight whispering sound, brushing against one another as they kept up that continued movement.

Once more we made a careful detour about their station. There came then a whole section of boxes holding nothing but the brittle bits of the dead. Above this a matching section of the bars held no light. We walked more freely here and the gars pushed forward

too, since they did not have to avoid the planted boxes.

I had no way of telling the time or how long we had been on the move—first into the Tangle, and then coming to this underground forcing house. However I believed that we all must rest. Illo agreed to that, not knowing what might lie ahead. Here among the empty earth boxes would be a safe place to camp. The gars, relieved of their burdens, lay down since there was no grazing for them. I spared each a cake of our own dried provisions and shaved a fourth into slivers which Illo and I chewed as we sat with our backs against one of the boxes.

Just as these had no lights above them, so did the drifting clouds of moisture appear to avoid passing directly over us. For which we were glad as we did not

fancy being suddenly rained upon. As I settled on my back and stared straight up into that "sky" I thought I could just distinguish, very far above the network of the light lines, a dark ceiling.

Illo did not settle down at once. Instead she burrowed into her pack, and, having turned over a number of small bags and bundles, she brought out a packet of what looked to be long, dried twigs. These she separated with care. Putting two to one side, she broke up a half dozen more into small lengths and then went to the gars, holding out first her palm on which rested some of the twig bits to Witol. He sniffed with an energy which nearly blew them away, then put out a purplish tongue, sweeping up what she offered. His companions seemed as eager to take their share.

When she came back she held out one of the two remaining twigs to me.

"This is arsepal. It has many virtues. Wild animals seek it out for themselves to chew upon. It strengthens, clears the senses, is a preventive of infections. I wish I had more of it. But I think it is well if we now follow a prudent course and do all we can to arm ourselves against any ill."

The root was aromatic, its scent, as I held it close to my nose, clean and clear against the dank, near-fetrid odors wafted from the growing beds. I chewed upon it and discovered, though it seemed to have no particular definable taste, it made my mouth feel clean. Also, once moistened by saliva, it softened, was easy to chew small and swallow.

She was not so quick to sample her own portion but continued to sit there, looking away from our small refuge by the dry and the dead towards the massed boxes before us where things grew far too luxuriantly to make me easy of mind. At that moment I did not want to look ahead, only lie and let the tiredness seep out of me in sleep—if one dared sleep in such a place.

"What are you thinking of?" I asked at last, mainly because I could not reach for that sleep with her still sitting there, a half-chewed twig in her fist and her eyes set on what I could not see. For I was sure she was no longer just watching the plants themselves.

"Of the link—" the words came from her with a force which aroused me. "What is the link—between what we have seen this day and the Shadow doom? Who first named it Shadow doom—and why? They might as well have spoken of lead death—of the Unknown—of—of—" her sentences trilled away as she still stared at what I could see, and perhaps, more at what I could not.

I had no answer for her, she did not even wait for one, but her words plunged on:

"Those flowers—they are the first proof of link. What reason for their being in the villages?" She flung her arms wide as if she would grasp something and pull it to her. "I want to know! I must know!" Then that trance-like stare broke and she glanced at me as if she saw me once again as a person. For the first time she smiled, her calm mask breaking so that in this alien place she was all human, not even a healer any more.

"When I was little," even the tone of her voice was changed, it had lost that faint hint of intoning, "I used

to read story tapes. There were all the old, old adventures which are still always new—probably because way back in time somewhere they did hold once a kernel of truth. There was always the lady in great distress, menaced by all manner of evil, from monstrous beasts to dark-hearted men. But through all her trials she never lost heart, always knew that good would finally triumph.

"Then there was the hero, a mighty fighter and doer, who did not know the very name of fear, and to whom danger was a challenge he went eagerly to meet. The two of them were plunged into all manner of action through which they fought with sword, or wit, or plain strength of arm until evil was overcome and good put on a victory crown.

"Sometimes I wondered what it would be like to be caught in such an adventure—" She paused and I cut in:

"So now you are and discover that the truth is somewhat different—one's feet ache from walking, one can feel the cold of fear, also that you do not have the support of knowing that it will all come right in the end. Yes, adventures are not what the tapes would have us believe." I deliberately settled my head on the pillow of my pack and closed my eyes. In truth I realized that I was no hero and certainly could not make a good showing as one, no matter how action might call for such an effort. I thought that there might be a hint of mockery in her talk—though I believed that was a show on her part, meant probably to bolster her own spirits. At that moment I was selfish enough to want to try and refresh my own. The last things I wished to consider were the attributes of a proper hero.

I was even tired enough to sleep, willing to depend upon the gars for sentry duty, since I knew that they never slept soundly, but spent their rest halts and nights in light doses, awakening at intervals to graze— even though there was no grazing here.

Night and day must be all the same here. I came awake later aware of a weight resting half against my arm. Bemusedly, not yet fully aroused, I turned my head a fraction and saw that Illo was huddled down beside me, not the width of a camp fire away, and her head had rolled against me. She was deep in sleep, her breath coming in slow even rhythm. Her face, however, had a frown line locked between her brows as if questions without answers still haunted her.

Gently I moved away from her, allowing her head to rest on the edge of my pack, as I slipped out from the half-weight of it. The light was the same; the gars still knelt chewing their cuds which must be near vanished by now. Witol opened his big eyes as I came up, and closed them again, having assured himself, I supposed, that all was well.

However, slowly I became aware that the peace which had appeared a part of my sleep no longer existed. Just as the nodding flowers had given us the feeling of being watched, so I sat up and looked around, surveying the long vistas of the aisles between the boxes, planted, or full of the dead, with a growing uneasiness. There was something here—even if the gars on which I had, perhaps foolishly, depended for sentries did not appear to sense any trouble.

Though I studied all, I could see there was no outward change—only the misty pseudo-clouds were ever in motion, all else was quiet and silent. Still that sense which is sharp in one who has lived on and with the plains got me to my feet, moved me to the next aisle to peer up and down—and then to the one beyond.

Here the lights glowed and that dangerous growth was vigorous. So I kept a careful distance from it, drawing the stunner, hoping that if I came under any attack I could face that as well here with the same weapon as had defeated the Tangle.

Here all was very quiet. Here I could not hear the breathing of the gars, the slight rustle Illo might be making turning in her sleep. It was as if I were totally alone, caught in strangeness, hedged about by alienness which was threatening because it had no possible meeting point with my own species.

In those moments that I stood there my view of this place shifted. I had considered it a forcing house for plants—perhaps an experimental station, such as my own kind used on other worlds to test the possibilities of adapting natural food products to strange soils. Only that logic was based on my observation and information. What if there was an entirely different reason for the forcing of the plants?

At that moment there crept into my mind, thin and weak at first, as might a first root break out of a seed casing, another conception altogether. There were no armies on Voor. My kind had never had to band together against a concrete and visible foe. I had never even seen any of the Patrol, the armed might of The Federation, except when once a cruiser on a routine outer fringe world flight had landed a squad at Portcity, mainly to pick up some records a disabled Survey ship had jettisoned there.

Since the Shadow doom had always remained just that—shadowy, unknown—one did not think of it as a trained force, an army. What the Voorloper had to fight he faced alone—weather such as the sudden storm which had been our bane, a handful of hostile animals, the mishaps of a sudden illness where there was no medical aid. These dangers would be small against—

My whole body tensed, my fingers ached a little with the tight grip I kept on the stunner which was ready, which, without my conscious volition, swerved slowly from side to side as if I were prepared to sweep free a broad path with my ray. Yet here was no tangle of jungle—there were the orderly networks of aisles leading to infinity. I wrangled my distance glasses loose with my left hand, keeping the stunner ready in the other.

Boxes, some full, some dead, a numberless procession of them, and that was only along the one aisle. I could not sight the far end of the place in which I stood because—

I blinked, wiped the lenses of the glasses against my thigh, put them to my eyes again. There *was* a definite limit, far from here—but no wall. Rather a thick mist, as if the small cloudlets overhead had their birth there, breaking from a greater mass which touched the floor.

And—

I began to back down the side aisle which had brought me away from my companions. I had not just imagined that! My eyes were too distance-wise to be deceived. The foggy mass was on the move, in our direction!

At the same time I made sure of that, I was swung

219

back against on the boxes, hurled off balance by a ring of fire about my throat. The glasses fell from my grasp as I threw up my hand to tear at the necklet. But I did not lose my hold on the stunner.

With that circle of pain eating into my flesh I was no longer Bart s'Lorn. Or rather I was he battling what I could not see, hear, feel, but which was in me. I must go forward—this was needful—I was—

Food?

The conception was such a shock that it broke the hold of the pressure on my brain. That small recession of struggle let me marshal my forces. I turned and staggered back, wavering from side to side, slamming with bruising force from the boxes on one edge of the walkway to those on the other.

The necklet did not feel hot to my fingers, but there was my own blood welling from the frantic scratches of my nails striving to pull it open.

"Bart—?"

Illo was pulling herself up to her feet with one hand on a box where brittle stems turned to powder at her touch. "Bart—!" Her eyes were large, staring at me as if I had suddenly put on a monster's mask. Then she fairly sprung away from the box to meet me; with both hands she caught mine as I clawed so futilely at the necklet.

It was Illo—truly it was Illo—not that other—that other with her mouth twisted open to voice a hideous scream. Dark hair—light hair—one face over another —and then gone again. I was going mad—the whole world was twisting around me, assuming one shape which melted into another, and then another—

There was a hag! No, she was not old—young,

young and evil, and her mouth gaped open to show teeth ready to tear wolfishly at my flesh. No—she was old—old with all the evil knowledge gained during a vicious life in those burning eyes, and she had a knife —a knife to match that which was already sawing at my throat.

She led the pack. I must get away—run— I brought up my fist and sent it crashing into her face. Then the face was gone. I could run—run to meet *them,* the others—those who waited—who needed me.

This was like trying to run through a viscous flood rising higher and higher about my legs. I was wading now. The level reached my knees, clung about my thighs. I could not see it! I threw out both hands, strove to cast the invisible off. My hands met nothing. Still it was there, slowing me down, holding me back so that they could catch me.

They—they were everywhere! There was no escape! My heart pounded in great jolts, trying to break through the cage of my ribs, tear its own path out of my body. The pain at my throat—my head was being forced up and back, a garrot might be slowly closing about my neck.

I screamed like a tortured animal:

"Almanic! Almanic!"

He was here somewhere. I had been loyal—I had carried the summons to the kin—I had obeyed orders —thus I deserved his help.

The tide of the mist—the death mist—rolling forward to meet me. Food—the cursed creations needed food. They had taken and taken—and taken—

"Almanic!"

It was hard to keep my feet with that sucking flood

rising about me. Ahead I could see them—the Outer Company—the defenders—I must reach them before the gate closed—I must!

Those others—storming at my heels, creeping in from the sides. This was their place, they knew it. The things they had spawned from their own black delving into the forbidden reached greedy tendrils for me.

A lashing out— I was jerked back, not by the cord about my neck, but that which hurled from one side, which tightened about my waist, crushing in about my body until pain was a red mist rising in my head, blotting out everything.

"Almanic!" I cried in despair. The gate was closing. I had fallen to my knees. There was none who dared leave his place and come to aid me. Too few—they were needed, needed to hold the sanctuary. To sacrifice themselves if the need came. I must watch all hope shut away.

But the eaters would not get me! Or else they would get my body when it no longer mattered. My key—my life key! My hands up to that.

"Ullagath nu ploz— " Words which would release me, by their tones alone, to a final dissolution. *They* could come upon me now but what would lie to their hands would be of no use to them— They must have their meat alive!

"—fa stan—" I must remember! Why did the proper words fade in and out of my mind? I had known them beyond any forgetting since I was old enough to wear a key as a man and a warrior. "—fa stan—"

What was next? By the Will of the Fourth Eye, what was next? I must have it! Now—before they cut me down, bound me, drew me back to serve their beastial appetites.

"—stan dy ki—" It was coming again—I must hold on. I realized dimly that my shoulder was jammed against a wall of some sort—that around me was an awful stench of death and decay—that that pressure about my middle was pulling tighter and tighter, until pain ran hot fingers up into my brain—I could not remember! I must!

"—ki nen pla—"

Someone was calling. Not the one of the Outer Company. They had gone, the gate was closed.

"Bart—!"

I shook my head. It troubled me, that word—a name—yes, it was a name. But it had no meaning! I must remember—

The pressure about my waist gave way. I sprawled forward, crashing hard against an unyielding substance. I could not remember—I would be meat, meant for the half-men! With a last dying hope I sought the bar resting against my throat. If I could only remember! Instead, I plunged into the dark— perhaps the Power was merciful after all, and I had gained death without the ritual, I thought, as I surrendered to that engulfing wave.

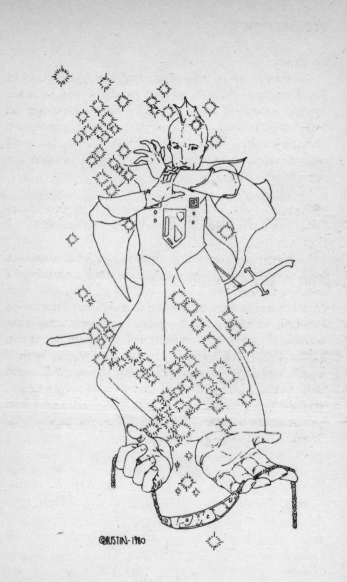

@AUSTIN-1980

12.

I was moving, but not on my feet—rather I half sat, half lay on the back of a living creature that bore me forward. There was a mist—a cloud which had seeped into my mind. I could not think. Who was I? The citadel had fallen and the half-people had loosed the growing death—fed it horribly. No! I dare not think! Let me slip back once more into that nothingness of non-memory—non-mind!

This body being borne forward—was not mine. Let me be free of it! Free—

I tried to move and found that I was a prisoner—in bonds. The half-men had taken me!

Then from my forehead there began to spread a coolness, driving back the fire which ate at me, in me. Very, very far away I heard sounds rhythmically repeated. Sounds?—words? Words which had no meaning—alien words. The half-men would lock me with their word spells, even as they had bound me with their living ropes. I tried to close my mind to those words—so to keep the ill in them from me. What was the chant of protection? I could not remember it! That

226

was gone, stripped from me, as a prisoner is stripped of all weapons. And still those sounds continued:

"Return—Bart, Bart, Bart—return!"

The coolness spreading into my head, waning, pouring over, smothering, the chaos whirling in my brain which would not let me think!

"Return—you are Bart s'Lorn! You are Bart s'Lorn. Awake and remember! Return—Bart s'Lorn!"

Bart—that was a name—a name I knew once. When and where? Who had he been? Some comrade-in-arms kinsman? Who—who?

If I could grasp the memory of Bart then I would have a key— A key—there had been a key, too— A key! A necklet which I wore! But that was mine—given me when I had become a man to serve—to serve—

My head was filled with pain worse than any hurt of body, as if a war raged in the very channels of my brain itself—as if two fought there in desperate battle.

"Bart s'Lorn! Wake, Bart—wake!"

The cool pressure on my head—that was not of the evil of the half-men. It was beneficient, healing— Healing? There had been one who was a healer. For just a moment it was as if a face, serene, untouched by any of the raging conflict I knew, was clear in my memory—a young face—the face of one who was a mender, not a destroyer.

"Bart—"

I was not only thought—I was also body. My body contained me—it must obey my commands. I was a person—I was— With a great forcing of will I made the body obey me. I opened my eyes.

The world about me was dim, fogged—as if the parts of this body answered only sluggishly to my will. See! I ordered—see, for me—now!

Now the fog broke. I could see! I was riding on the back of a large animal. Only I was not alone. There was one who sat behind me on that broad back, whose hands were up, pressed against my forehead. It was from them that the blessed healing coolness reached into me.

More and more of the space around us cleared to my sight. We rode down an aisle between beds of vegetation, keeping an exact middle path. For from those beds arose whips of vine tentacles which reached vainly to ensnare us, flowers the color of open wounds leaned far forward seeking to engulf our flesh—to feed —to smother—to kill!

"Bart!" She whom I could not see, who rode behind me, called that name yet once again. The touch of her hands upon my head tightened, but not with that terrible compelling pressure I had known in the earlier assault which had sent me whirling thankfully into the dark.

I drew a deep breath; I began to understand at last. Though I had been—somewhere else—and I had *been* —been another—I was truly who she now hailed: Bart s'Lorn. Even as I knew that, the other identity in me made a last despairing attack, but this time her touch gave me strength to hold.

"Illo!" I cried her name, and that was another key, unlocking more of the past. My task was like trying to patch the holes in a tattered strip of weaving, so that the design would once more be whole and right.

"Bart!" There was a joyful note now in her answer.

Though I could not see her face, I thought that she was triumphant—that I had fulfilled some task she had longed for me to accomplish by my own efforts.

Task? For a moment only that other gave a last shadowy cry of thought—the task—duty—I had *failed!* Only that was not so—I was here, in the here and now —I was Bart s'Lorn!

Slowly I found words, but, as I spoke aloud, my voice sounded weak as might that of one who had been ill a long time.

"What happened?"

"You were not yourself," she answered promptly. "I do not know what or who possessed you. You said that we must reach the Gate before we were taken. One of the vines caught you. I stunned it free—and then we got on Witol and we rode. I have been trying to draw you back. And who is Almanic? You called that name many times."

"Almanic—" I repeated. Yes, once more a shadow thought curled quickly and was gone before I could seize it. "I think he was a friend but also a war leader, I believe he was the one who ordered me— No, not *me* —but perhaps he who once wore this necklet—to do something. And the wearer was too late."

I was still weak inside, but I could now see clearly. We were still transversing one of the aisles, though here all the boxes were planted with vigorous growth, growth which moved and twisted as we rode by. I knew the reason for that unnatural life and it set me shivering.

"What is the matter?" Illo demanded instantly. Her hands were no longer pressed against my forehead, but rested, one on each of my shoulders, as if it were necessary that she keep close contact with me.

"They fed—these things were fed—on—flesh and blood! This was the place—no, I cannot remember!" Nor did I want to. Save that, in me, the cold horror grew stronger and stronger. I had to fight with all the will power I could summon to keep myself from sheer panic.

"Do not try!" Her command was sharp. Once more her hands were on my forehead, and, with her healer's skill, she drove away that evil out of me.

I looked steadily ahead. There had been a thick mist there—surely I remembered that now. The cloudlets still floated overhead, but the fog which had been so dense when I last remembered surveying the far part of this garden (if one can call such a forcing place that) was gone. I did not know how far we had come, but before us now was a doorway—a closed doorway.

There were plants as tangled there as they had been in the splotch of upper jungle. I had a queer, fleeting impression that once they had swarmed here as a tide, trying to beat a way through that portal. A great patch of them spread out from that to the right, forming a thick river of growth which reached up and up, past the network of lights, a column steady now with the matted substance of seeking vegetation standing against the wall to reach out—up and out!

However it was toward the door they guarded we headed.

As at the open portals we had seen there was a curved arch carrying the intricate unreadable script of the unknown. I eyed the mass of vegetation warily.

"The stunner, where is it?"

"Here," once more her hands dropped from my

forehead. A moment later she reached around before me with the weapon. I checked its charge. The unit was full.

"I used the last of the other one." Illo explained, "to ray that vine which was squeezing you to death. It is recharged but we have only two more charges."

I made the setting carefully, adjusting it from wide to a narrower beam. Witol paused just beyond the reach of the waving vines and branches. Here the plants were far more active, greedy, demanding. They were larger, too, with a bloated look to them.

Squeezing the button I sent the first ray at a particularly active vine which had twice lashed at us, only to sprawl short by just a fraction, not knowing whether this weapon would still serve us. The vine jerked as might a man who had taken a hit. Then it looped limply down, and those behind it also started to wither. Encouraged, I played the ray back and forth across the whole width of the door, watching the mass droop and die.

Our path open, Witol walked forward of his own accord. Then, from the centermost point of the door arch, there suddenly shot a finger-thin beam of blue light. It struck, full on my throat, at the necklet.

From out of the air above us sounded a voice, with the inflection, I thought of a question. Password—? Was escape to be locked against us by the safeguards set eons ago?

The necklet was once more warm. While from somewhere, perhaps out of the nightmare of that other mind which had invaded mine, I picked words—two of them—meaningless sounds—still I was as sure of their importance as if I had been taught them from earliest childhood:

"Iben Ihi!"

There came a groaning, a shivering of the door. The leaves grated apart slowly, so slowly—opening to us. Twice I thought it was stuck and would move no farther. Perhaps Illo and I could have scraped through that thin slit but the gars, no. And there was no thought of leaving them.

On it went by jerks, the scraping loud. At last we had space enough. Witol walked forward without being urged, and we came out of that place of evil growth into a long corridor which inclined upwards at a gentle slope.

The corridor was not clear. Men had died here, or things with the bony likeness of men. They lay full length upon the floor or in piles along the walls as if they had leaned there until time had sent their bones sliding down. Armor of metal were about some of the bodies, and I noted all I could see clearly wore about their neck bones collars like that which chance had set upon me.

There were weapons, too, or at least I judged some rods, a few still clasped by finger bones, to be those. We did not stop to examine this battlefield. I had a vast reluctance to look at the dead, an aversion to disturbing their rest. Even Witol picked his way with care, striving not to touch one of the sprawling piles of bones.

Our way was lighted by a soft diffusion of gray, though I could see no torches, none of those criss-cross rods of illumination which had been in the large plant chamber. Witol was unable to quite avoid touching one outflung skeleton arm. At contact the bones crumbled into a white powder, an armlet of metal fell, with a soft small clang, to the floor. Though the air was fresh enough there was such a feeling of both age and despair about this place that I was in a hurry to be past the ranks of the dead, to find the end of our road, only hoping that would be a door to the outer world.

For the first time since we had entered this way Illo spoke:

"What were those words—those with which you commanded the door? I have heard off-world tales of doors and enclosures where a barrier is set to open only to certain sounds, some only if one certain imprinted voice utters them. But this is no off-world place of our time—"

"I do not know. Somehow they were just in my head," I had to answer. Her surmise concerning the reason for the opening door sounded logical to me. There is no guarantee that what has been discovered by one race or species in the past may not be recovered by those who follow them long after. Doors, safe keeping boxes, and files, on my world at Portcity could be sealed by the thumb of their owner thrust into a sensitive opening, one attuned only to that owner.

At that moment I was willing to believe that those who had fashioned this installation (whatever they had intended it to be) could have sealed the secret of some of their doors into the necklet. That confronted by the voice demanding the proper password some locked-in simulator had produced in my mind the proper words. So far we had been amazingly lucky. I could only hope (for what that hope might be worth) that this luck would continue.

The slowly rising ramp was not long and was

topped by another door. This one lacked that arch and inscription, but as Witol advanced, with more confidence than I could summon, it too, as if in answer to our very approach began to open with the same grating reluctance the others had shown.

I heard Illo's soft gasp of wonder as the opening split middle of that door grew wider. We were looking into a place lighted as had been the garden hall, but with a less strident, more eye-easy glow. And what did we see? Was it the equivalent of one of our villages, or a large holding, of even Portcity? Or was it simply one large complex of living and working quarters all linked, still quartered here and there by passages, such as that which lay beyond the door?

The buildings were not of the metal which had been in common use elsewhere, but rather of another substance, almost as if one had gathered great gleaming jewels and hollowed them, giving them doorways. They were of different shapes, which added to the gem simulance. Some were square and tabled with recessed step cutting, some carbochon, ovals, or drops, other sharply pointed, diamond fashion. Colors played across them, ebbing and flowing, though each had one color particularly its own and the ebb and flow was the darkening and lighting of shades of that color.

Though I have seen tapes made of the pleasure worlds, and some of the remains of fabulous Forerunner finds, I had never seen the like of these. It was like viewing a dream world. One felt that a single step forward into the valley which ran ahead might break that dream, shatter those fantastic jewels into nothingness.

There were no clouds overhead, nor any visible grid

been set, in scattered pattern, circles of crystal, as if to represent the stars of the outer world. None of these were bright enough to emit any true light, and I guessed that that must be diffused from the buildings, or even the walls of this huge cavern.

Whether the city holding hollow had been formed by nature or by the efforts of intelligence I could not guess, but it seemed to be a half-sphere, the walls we could see sloping up in that fashion. There was no sign of any growing thing, again in sharp contrast to the perilous way we had come. The silence was awe-inspiring and complete. So complete, that the hoof clicks of Witol and the other gars sounded far too loud, somehow wrong, as if this wondrous place should have been left to drowse eternally, dreaming—

I had half expected to see more evidence here of whatever disaster had struck down those defenders within the outer portal. However the way or street before us was bare. If any dead remained, they lay within their homes and I had no desire to explore there. In fact both Illo and I were content to stay on Witol's back as the bull paced proudly forward.

Our feeling of intrusion slowly died, but not our sense of wonder at the beauty of the place. There was no sign of any aging, no evidence here of disaster or defeat.

Illo spoke very softly, as if any voice might disturb some sleeper:

"Their end—it came well."

When I made no answer, she said:

"Can you not feel it? The peace? All that was dark and evil shut out forever?"

My hands without my conscious willing went to the

necklet. That was still as warm as the skin on which it lay. Far back in my mind swirled once more that terror and horror which I had carried with me into the darkness—swirled, died—was gone. I could feel now as she did that there was nothing here—not the dead awesome silence of Mungo's Town and Voor's Grove, the menace of the Tangle—that other stranger and more fearsome terror which had lain in wait among the planted boxes. No—there was not an emptiness which made a man feel estranged and alien—there was peace—utter peace.

Illo's sensitivity, born from her talent, had felt it first, now it spread to me. I did not believe that this wondrous jeweled city had been deserted by those who had rejoiced in its beauty. Rather they had made a choice, withdrawn into their homes, accepted freely, with thankfulness and wistful longing, that final peace.

Witol paced on, but the clicking of gars' hooves could never disturb the sleepers here. We passed between the ever-changing hues of the walls until we came to one structure which bore no color at all. It was crystalline, yet its shape was wrought in facets as a gem might well be treated to best display its finest qualities.

The gar bull came to a halt. Looking about I judged that this crystal of many flickering sparks of fire was the center of the alien city. For here the streets, or ways, between the smaller structures converged to join in a circle about it.

Three spires of the flashing substance arose above all other of the buildings and there was a wide open entrance before us. I slid from Witol's back, reached up and drew Illo down with me. That we had reached the heart of all the mysteries which had been set to plague us and our kind—I was as sure of that as if I had shouted aloud some question and had been answered with the weight of true authority.

We would discover no sleepers here, of that I was also sure, as I went up the two broad, wide steps which raised the diamond walls above the rest. With Illo's hand in mine I stepped confidently forward into what? A temple raised to some unknown force for good (for such a place as this could not house evil), a meeting place of assembly like our village halls, the palace of some ruler? It could be any one or all three.

We passed within where sparks of light appeared to dance in the air. There was something else too, which made me alert, clear of mind, free from all fatigue of body, insecurity or doubt. This was how man was meant to feel—always and ever!

I turned my head a little. Illo's eyes met mine. In them was my wonder mirrored, heightened, made into pure joy. We gazed at each other for a long moment. Something in me demanded that I hold to this, hold fast—for this was a moment which meant much. It would mean even more if one had that in him which could rise to the greater heights—the mountain tops of self-knowledge and confidence these others knew. Only—even as I realized that, I knew that my species was not made for such heights. We were as cracked jugs into which poured spring water, fresh and clear, only to have that dribble forth little by little, leaving us empty ever more.

Hand in hand we went on between lines of flashing pillars until we came to the centermost heart of the place, even as it was the heart of the city. There was a

238

bowl of opaline substance, around its sides also traveling rainbow fires. Only here those were softened, made less dazzling, less brilliant.

We looked down into that and saw that in the very bottom, where that bowl was the deepest, there was liquid, a small, still pool of it, perhaps one cupful, or at the most two. As the bowl which held it, it showed many colors which skimmed its surface, now blue, now gold, now green, now red—now all mingled together in a burst of radiance.

Illo dropped my hand and fell to her knees, her hand stretched forward, reaching down, until her forefinger tips touched the water. She sang, low, soft, words I could not understand. Yet I never wanted her to stop, for the singing was the color, the brilliant, ever changing color, and the color was the singing. Though what I meant by that I could not make plain even to myself.

Slowly I, too, knelt. My hands were once more on the necklet. This time, as I fingered the plate set against the hollow of my throat there sounded a chime. Unlike Illo's singing that did not mingle with the color, but was apart, and it gathered in it both paeans of triumph, despair of defeat.

The necklet fell forward, was loose in my hand. I held it so, knowing what I must do with it. There could be no troubling of this peace. The last loose thread of the pattern must be returned to the weaver and bound fast. I leaned forward, allowed the necklet to slip into the pool.

No longer was the water still. The liquid began to churn about, rising as though I had taken a kettle ladle and stirred it so. Rise it did, higher and higher; faster it flew about the sides of the bow, until one could not

see water at all, only streamers of color whipped about, beaten into one another, emerging once again. Nor could I turn my eyes away from that whirl, though I knew the sight was setting a compulsion on me, preparing me for—

I was in a garden and there was a woman singing as Illo had sung, soft and low, and very happy. She was setting out small plants one by one, packing rich earth about their roots. There was the warmth of sun in the air and I was very happy. We were going to the fair and I would be able to buy some toy for my own self. I had my precious coin in my belt purse. I could feel it through the stuff of that purse whenever I pinched, and I pinched many times over.

If she would only hurry—this was no day for planting in the garden—it was festival time. I ran to the edge of the street to look and listen. The street was very wide, the houses tall—or else I was small.

Then—

It was as if a dark cloud had crossed the sky. That cloud broke into pieces, and those pieces were dropping, raining down upon us. I was afraid and I cried and ran, ran inside the house, and hid my face against a cloth on the table. I heard cries, gasps. Then I knew there was something in the room with me. Fear struck me into a small tense statue. I dared not look—yet I must—it was forcing me to look— No!

Maybe I screamed, perhaps my throat was too taut with terror to let me make a sound. It was calling me, making me—I had to—

I turned, bringing handfuls of the table cloth in my grasp.

What stood there—for the second time in my life I

attempted to blot it out—but this time I could not do so.

Those flowing, swirling outlines of the figure tightened, its substance became more opaque. Yet, though it had a pseudo-human form, it was not a person. Young as I was I knew a jolting terror of what I saw forming under my eyes, making its own body from bits of leaf, the flyaway seeds of plants I had played with in the garden, other seeds, some still in their pods, nuts in their shells and out—

It stood hunched a little, and it had hands, now tightened, thickened so that the fingers, crooked like claws, were as solid as my own. Thorns instead of nails crowned each of those fingers. Only it was not just the threat of those reaching for me which caused me to scream, to back until my small body was flat against the wall so I flung up an arm to ward it off.

I called for my mother, for my father. My throat was raw with the force of my screams. No one came—only that—that *thing* which had holes in its face where the eyes should have been. Still, even if there were no eyes, it could see me. It stretched forth one arm, that thorn clawed hand, but it did not try to touch me. Rather those fingers crooked in a beckoning gesture.

I had folded my body closer to the floor, a small animal, nearly stark-crazed with fear. It did no good to scream any longer, I knew that dimly. Now I was so stricken with fright I was easy prey; still it came no closer. Twice it beckoned. I did not move. There was a prickling feeling in my head, I knew that it was calling me, expecting me to follow, to come to it.

My body even stirred as if to obey. Now I balled myself, my face hidden on my knees, my arms

wrapped about my head and shoulders. I was retreating from that horror, retreating into my own self, deeper and deeper. I would *not* look!

The special horror of the thing which I felt dimly, even as I made the plunge into an inner darkness, was that it had made itself—made its form out of things I knew, had handled, had played with. It was to me as if the wall of a room had formed a mouth to suck me in—window eyes to watch me. All my world in those moments took on a fearsome otherness I was not prepared to face, and which was so utterly alien I had to blot it out of my mind as well as hide it physically from my sight. For to have the familiar change before one's eyes into a frightening otherness was such an ordeal that perhaps even an adult would have found hard to face.

Darkness, and then suddenly it was light and I was under a warm sun, riding perched high on a gar's back. By the side of the beast paced my father, his face set, white under the weathering, the lines upon it the signature of some horror looked upon and never to be wholly faced. I had returned again to memory—my first memory. Yet now I had, at last, reached behind that to know a fraction of what shock had veiled from me all these years.

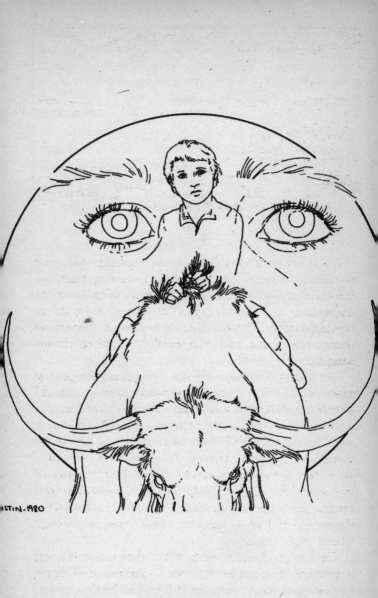

13.

I blinked and blinked again. There was no gar—nor my father. A sense of loss filled me for a long moment, then seeped away. I stood and watched liquid churn up and up in an opaline bowl of a pool. My past retreated farther and farther, to become a picture of something which had happened to another person long ago.

Yet, though my memory was still incomplete, out of some hidden corner came answers—slowly—one by one. The colors in the pool met, mingled, became other shades, darker, lighter, took on patterns. I had seen such lines and swirls before—yes! My hand flew to my throat. Then I remembered that that alien chain was gone, that I had hurled it into that same pool where it had sunk into hiding. Only those lines of color were much like those which had patterned the foreplate, those which had been over the doorways through which we had passed.

The designs had meaning. What they would tell was important, imperative for me to understand! Some buried emotion in me raged and fought for that understanding. I dropped to my knees and flung out my hands. Spatters of foam, raised by the faster and faster passage of the water being stirred around and around, struck my fingers, dripped from my outstretched palms.

I withdrew those wet hands, brought them to my face, my forehead, pressed flesh against flesh with the water in between. Straightway I became aware of a sharp scent filling my nostrils, making even my closed eyes smart and begin to tear.

However that same water—or the scent of it— cleared my head, shook me into such a sharp awareness as I had never quite known before. I dropped my hands, shook my head from side to side, yet again blinking my eyes to clear them of the tears that scent or strength in the liquid had induced.

I stared down into the massing and the flowing of the color. This was part of a talent, or else some strange science of a race long forgot, utterly alien. So that the messages they had left—the warnings—came through to a mind such as mine only in fragments and broken phrases.

Piece by piece I fought to catch a hint here, an almost entirely clear reading there. My people depended upon tapes for their records; what I was watching now was something like those in its results but very unlike in substance. There were so many holes that I had to bridge the message by leaps of imagination, by flights of guessing.

Two races—one from space, a remnant fleeing some unexplained disaster out among the stars. Each of another culture, so divided in ways of logical thought pattern that communication between the natives and the star-rovers was near impossible.

Yet those natives had taken in the refugees, tried hard to make their settlement prosper. Greed, drive for domination, were taints the star-rovers carried like foul diseases in their blood. The taking over of knowledge peculiar to the people of this planet consisting in the main of their extraordinary talents for shaping and control of plants, their oneness with all forms of life on their world. The newcomers seizing upon their knowledge, yes, but not learning the strict controls imposed by a high moral sense.

Experimentation to adapt the growth of this new world to the service of the newcomers—experiments which were used in excess and misused. Plants which became like mind-changing drugs—an unruly and anarchic people addicted to them—the need for more and more—

War, for the natives learned too late the manner of the race they dealt with, the horrors which could be loosed with forced mutation gone mad.

Plants deliberately fed—on flesh, on blood, on living bodies. The result of such deaths—the Shadows. Things with tenacious life but which were greed, hunger, born from engorged plants as near wisps of nothingness, needing to build new bodies by their will from fragments of leaves, seed, even earth dust. Development of raging hunger, until that changed into a potent weapon to draw to the feaster, walking, living food!

Immortality for the shadow being in a fashion. Development at last of creatures so alien that they had no possible contact even with that which had been their own source. Resting dormant between the feedings, yet awaking when the food, the rich feasting again landed in Voor. The gathering of energy—slow at first —then richer, fuller, stronger as the Shadows went forth, bursting from their seed cases where they had lain waiting for time, past our counting of years.

Shadows who had no substance until they could make themselves bodies, but with wills so compelling that they could call to them, bring into their nesting boxes their food.

The natives—so great had been their horror at what they had unleashed, they had chosen a final withdrawal, leaving only a record which might never be read—the record lying before our eyes—an accusation and a warning.

"So—that is it!"

Words startled me, broke the chain of communication between me and what was to be read in the pool. I looked to Illo. Her face was starkly pale beneath the weathering brown; there was such a sickness in her face that I moved quickly to steady her where she also had knelt to stare into the pool.

"They—they—ate our—own people!" The horror in her voice was a sick cry. Her mouth twisted as I pulled her into my arms, her face now hidden against my shoulder.

I felt my own stomach churn, a sourness rising in my throat, I could not put out of my mind that line of skeletons. Then they—*they* had been so long from food, so starving—they had not brought back their prey as they had done from other settlements but had—*feasted* there! I retched, fought my nausea. Illo was shuddering in my hold.

"Don't!" her cry was muffled against my shoulder.

"Don't!"

I hoped she had not in some manner (nothing seemed impossible to me here and now) read my thoughts. Perhaps she was fighting terrible memories of her own.

"Did you remember?" I asked between those waves of nausea which I battled.

"Yes—" her voice was very faint. Her fingers dug into my shoulders, scraped together, in a frantic hold, handfuls of my jerkin.

"Why not us—?" The one question which the pool had not answered. Why had we escaped?

"We—we were—we were fed on the food of this world from birth, we were *of* Voor—there was a kinship—a faint kinship—between us and—*them!*"

I shuddered. If her answer was the truth I could easily come to loathe myself.

"No!" again it was as if she could read my thoughts. "Not for us in truth. They—*they* chose to change. But they could still recognize—maybe without knowing it —those bred here. Perhaps they wanted us to join them—to renew—to be with them!"

I remembered that *thing*, its thorn-clawed hands which had not torn me but rather had beckoned. Dim kinship? A need to add fresh life to its dreadful company? Had that indeed moved it?

"One of them could have taken me—easily," I said slowly. It had been a thing all shaped from bits and pieces of vegetation, but it had looked solid enough. And certainly the activities of it and its fellows— I swallowed once, and again, still fighting that need to vomit.

"It had chosen." Illo turned her head a little so she

could look up to me. There were tear tracks down her face. "In the past it had chosen—perhaps such a choice always had to be made. They could invite—but such as we had to make the choice." She spoke as if she had complete belief in what she said. Whether that was the truth or not we might never know.

"This can't go on." I made myself turn from memories of the past. Sick as I was, resolve now filled me, pushing out the horror, stiffening my purpose.

Blasters? No. Those had been already tried and had failed— The things which we had sought, perhaps must seek again, to fight, were indeed shadows. The stuff of their bodies—when they needed bodies—could be summoned at their wills. But who can blast a shadow? The whole of the Tangle perhaps might be rooted up and destroyed by some weapons from off world. I did not doubt that the Patrol could bring in superior devices we had not even heard of. But none would prevail against shadows.

"Look—" Illo's grasp on me tightened, she drew me closer to the edge of the pool.

The intertwining race of colors and shades there was thinning. There remained only one bright thread clear running—the blue of the necklet's glow.

"Watch—" but she did not have to tell me that.

In and out, convolutions and spirals, in loops and double loops, it wound and unwound. Again there was so much I could not understand, that I could only guess.

Those who had withdrawn to their gem-bright city, had locked their gates, and then chosen of their own will to pass on into another existence, had left this message. Warning? Suggestion? It was both, though I

could be sure of so very little of it.

Then it had been beyond their abilities to do this thing themselves without becoming like the vile things they fought. Long dead now, they could not be degraded, used— Yet the Shadows retaining wisps of memory, their abiding hate for those who had defeated them, sentenced them to a long dormant waiting until our own people had come—the Shadows would answer a call, catch at a chance avidly, thirsting to feast on what was no longer there but which to them was no memory, still existed.

Swarming in upon this last safe citadel so long inviolate they could be—eliminated. Or so the message came to me as I watched, more quickly to Illo—perhaps because her talent made her far more sensitive, while the necklet had in a measure built a lesser bridge of communication for me.

The girl pulled free of me and sped across the innermost chamber, back the way we had come. I followed her, not catching up until she stood on the top of those two wide steps which led to the pillared chamber.

"Look!"

The gars had come up to us, turned, their heads low, tossing from side to side as they do when about to defend themselves against attack. Her gesture pointed beyond them.

There was a swirling in the air, visible only because some particles of glittering dust, perhaps all that time had shaken from the jewel buildings, writhed and danced in the air. There were no leaves, no bits of vegetation here which the invisibles could draw to them, yet they fought to shape something with what little did exist.

I could not number them, for there was no one swirl completely apart from the other. Illo hesitated only a moment and then swung about—I knew what was in her mind—there had been a final defense which the natives had set to protect their death sleep.

"The pool!"

That defense must have been activated by now, I realized that perhaps we would be caught in what was to come. What Illo would do I had no idea. That instinct which is in all of us to search for some way out when danger faces one did awake in me.

"Witol!" I caught at the nearest horn of the bull, "In!"

He bellowed, pawed the stone underfoot as if determined to stand his ground, then came, herding his mate and Wobru before him. We fairly fled between the rows of pillars back to the pool.

There were no longer any blue streamers racing across it. Still the liquid had not sunk back into the small cupfuls we had found there at our first coming. Rather the whole was taking on a red hue, a red shot through with sparks of orange and yellow—if fire could become water, then that was what we saw.

The flow reached the rim of the pool, the center going higher, forming a great bubble. Those orange and yellow lights disappeared, the stuff was thicker, viscid, darker red. I could think only of a giant welling of blood—

"Watch Witol!" Illo drew my attention from that terrible flood with a cry.

The gar bull had not paused at the pool, but was trotting on, still herding his two companions before him, uttering short bellows. I caught Illo by the hand and ran after the gars who now broke into the gallop which they could show when there was need, my strides lengthening as I attempted to catch up. All my Voorloper sense returned to me then. "Trust your gars" was the old and well-attested cry of the plainsmen.

We passed down another line of pillars, were in the street once more on the other side of that central shine. Witol galloped, Illo and I ran. The gars were mute now as if they did not want to waste their breath.

More of the gem houses flashed by us. What goal Witol might have I could not guess. Having no solution myself I was content to trust his instinct, always so much sharper than my own.

We came to another gate, another door. This time I had no necklet to guide me. But that same cry I had uttered to bring us here came to my lips again.

"Iben Ihi!"

The grating noise was louder, the portal showed only a few inches of opening then froze. Witol seemed to go mad. Lowering his head, the bull drew back a little and charged, the sound of the impact of his horns against the door ringing in echoes and re-echoes through the city of the dead.

The force which he had used must have jolted free the ancient mechanism for the door sprang open just as I thought his assault might have jammed it past any further effort. Witol whipped through that aperture with a speed one would not expect from his bulk, the other two crowding behind him. Illo raced, her one hand twisted in the lashing of the gear on Wobru's back, I was only seconds behind.

I looked back; the door was snapping shut even as I watched, once more sealed. We were on a ramp, a stepped ramp, leading up. The gars strained to take that incline at the same burst of speed.

Their instinct was keener than mine, yes, but now I, too, felt that warning. I had no idea what fate the long dead had left to be visited upon the enemy should they reach this final stronghold. But that it was drastic and complete I could well guess.

We scrambled and climbed. This had been no easy entrance nor exit such as the other ways. Here the smooth metallic coating had become rough stone, the stuff of Voor itself which acted to our advantage, for I doubt whether we could have climbed so fast on a smooth surface at such a sharp rising angle.

What light showed us the way ahead was very faint, once the gate was shut and the glittering of the city gone. There were only some grayish gleams at the head of the ramp. Witol had been forced to slacken speed by the steepness of the incline; he was snorting and panting now, but he did not falter.

Even as he had charged the gate, so now he drew a little ahead and butted at a mass of fallen stone which near sealed us in, except for crevices which allowed daylight through. Stones and earth flew, fell back on us. Witol made a last lumbering leap and was gone, the other two gars after him, bringing us along as we clung to the pack lashing.

I had expected to burst forth in the Tangle. Instead we were in a very narrow valley, a knife-edged cut between two ridges of rough rock. Witol, breathing hard, did not pause, though his speed was more labored, his panting near as loud as his grunts. He kept on down the middle of the narrow way, though that required scrambling over slides of fallen rock, a weaving in and out to find footing at all. There was no sign of any vegetation here—only grey rock seamed up the sides of that cut with wide bands of black which was like that from which the eyeless statue had been hewn.

If there had ever been any road here it was long since hidden under those slides. In fact so rugged were our surroundings, I would have thought that none could have ever forced a path here before.

We were at the end of the knife-narrow valley, then out into the beginning of a wider space in which there was a sparse growth of grass, when the blast came—with force enough to knock us from our feet, send rocks

crashing down all along the way we had come. The gars voiced such cries as I had never heard the beasts give before; their terror was plain. They ran on in a mad way, twice more being knocked from their feet by great earth shocks. Illo and I lay where the first of those had flung us, our fingers biting into the dusty earth to provide the only anchorage in what had become a shaken and shaking world.

I buried my face in the crook of my arm, coughing heavily, for dust arose to whirl so much about us it was a cloud to hide all—even my own hand lying so close to my face. The grit stung my eyes until they watered.

This then was the final answer of those in the

gemmed city—and we had loosed it. I was as sure of
that as if some voice out of the dust proclaimed our
deed aloud in a solemn indictment. The opening of the
gate where that hellish garden grew was invitation to
the Shadows to reach the prey they had always cov-
eted. Perhaps the essence of what made up the shadow
cores had no longer real intelligence, as well as no
body unless they built such—but I was certain that the
age-old hatred had not been lost.

Those skeletons we had found within the city gate—
had they been the last victims before somehow, with
their unknown knowledge, the natives had been able to
expel their enemies? I had a half thought which again

made sickness rise in my throat—volunteers? Men who had gone to such a death that satiated the victors, rendered the attackers so sluggish after their feeding, they could be better dealt with? We would never know —I did not want to.

But the city—its people driven to their final refuge had made their choice. They must not have been able to handle an attack in force—perhaps there had been only a handful of them left. Perhaps they had never lived or wanted to live on the outer surface of Voor. Only they had made sure that if their defenses were breached they would take the enemy with them. I—I had in reality been the one to breach the defenses— open the gate with the necklet which was the key.

Had the return of that to the pool not only released the final message, but also triggered the defense to ready, so that when the Shadows followed us greedy for the feast they were met with—?

With what? That there had been a mighty explosion underground was so evident it was not even necessary to speculate about that. However was any explosion enough to finish that which could not be seen, which had no substance unless it wished for it? Had we, instead of defeating the evil, loosed it instead, sent it free to roam with the wind?

My sickness grew stronger as I made myself face that possibility. My hope was a thin one—the city people had known the nature of their enemy. Certainly any final defense they would rig would be one which that nature could *not* withstand. Only hope is a tricky thing on which to build confidence.

Muffled by the dust I heard the bellow of the gars. It seemed to me that there was no fear in that sound any more—rather anger—and perhaps confidence. At least the ground had stopped shaking. There was still a rattle of falling stones, a crash of larger boulders in the vent valley from which we had emerged just in time. The dust was beginning to settle.

I sat up, trying to wipe my eyes without getting any more grit into them. My body was grey with dust. I coughed, and spit, choked, and coughed again. A figure thoroughly muffled in dust was performing like action an arm's length or so away.

Slowly I edged around without even getting up as far as my knees, for I had an uneasy feeling that if I tried that I would not stay even so far above the ground for long. The shifting billows of dust had fallen well enough to show me that there was no longer any break in the cliff wall. That crack through which we had run to safety was so choked now with rubble that it was sealed as tightly as a stopper could be pounded into a water bottle—

A water bottle!

The need for a drink struck me like a blow. Now I did get slowly, and with caution, to my knees, arose to stand, swaying, shielding my eyes against yet moving clouds of dust, looking out into the wide open land of grass and far spreading space. Not a tree, not a hint of bush, vine or thorn growth arose there. I licked dust from my lips and then wished that I had not, for it added to my thirst.

The other dust-covered figure which was Illo also stood up, weaving a little. Before us was the open land —not only that but I caught sight, through my watering eyes, of a greyish strip set in a lone thread of greenery, as if the growth there had not yet been season killed. The warmth which had been with us so that we had come to take it for granted, even as does a man the summer sun, ever since we moved along the edge of the Tangle was gone, cut off with a blast of chill wind against our backs.

I could see more clearly now—that ribbon was water and the humps moving determinedly towards it must be the gars. There was no other moving thing, nor even tallish growth. This was a land as stripped as the mid-plains I had known for most of my life.

"Come—!" I took one step and then another, and found that truly the ground was no longer rolling under me. I could walk. I need only cover the distance now lying between myself and that ribbon and water was mine.

Laying a supporting arm about Illo's shoulders, I started that march. We wavered together for a step or two and then strength flowed back into us, seeming to come the faster as we determinedly followed the gars into the open, nor did either of us look back.

My full attention was on reaching the water I craved, and we exchanged no words as we made that leg of our journey. Not until we threw ourselves full length in an opening between the stream-seeking bushes of a thicket and laved our faces, hands, arms, drank, rested and drank again, did she speak:

"It must be gone—all of it." Though I noticed she did not turn her head to look along our back trail to that valley which had ceased to be the last door to the underworld. "That was their final plan—if *those* got into the city to destroy it all!"

I rolled over on my back and lay looking up into the dun grey of the sky. It must be nearing twilight, but the roof of clouds overhead made it hard to judge. We should round up the gars, assemble our camp. Yes— that dark thought crept into my mind once more and clung.

"How," I blurted out, "do you destroy something which is only a—shadow?"

"*They* knew." Now Illo did turn her head a fraction, reluctantly, as if she must make herself do this. "It was by their arts that the first evil came to be; I think they had a last drastic control. While they lived they were not forced to use it. I think it would have been very hard for them to destroy their city—it was part of them."

"You talk as if you know—but how *can* you!" I persisted.

She was sleeking back the damp locks of her hair which had fallen into the water moments earlier and were now plastered into a ragged frame about her face, a face which seemed thinner, older, more tired than I had ever seen it.

"I know—" she hesitated as if hunting for words to make plain, emphatic what she would say— "I know it here!" The fingers of both of her hands were on her forehead just above her eyes, rubbing back and forth as if to ease some pain—or memory of pain. "It was in me—first the calling as I told you—that was true. And when the calling stopped and I believed that Catha must be dead—there was still a need in me—another calling, deeper buried, but one, I think which would have kept me crawling forward on my knees when I could no longer walk, if that had been necessary. That —all of it is gone!"

"You—" I remembered, but now it was not so hor-

rible, so immediate—rather as if time had raised the barrier between memory and this moment which it would have naturally done had all been normal in my world, "you were being summoned still—by Shadows?"

She was frowning and rubbing still at the frown lines as if to erase them.

"Perhaps, or perhaps something else. Perhaps it was time that certain conditions must be fulfilled. There was no real reason why we, of all travelers, should have stumbled upon the necklet—"

I sat up and drew my knees close to my chest, lacing my arms about them. Out of my inborn desire for independence I did not want to follow her reasoning. That was born of her talent, I told myself. Still there

were oddities about the both of us. Alone on Voor, as far as I knew, we were the only survivors of the Shadow doom. There had been that freak storm, the worst I had ever encountered in all my years on the plains, my father's death, the task he had laid on me.

Men who worship some forces greater than they themselves can truly imagine may see patterns in the laying out of our lives, reasons for action or choices which we do not understand. As if we are tools, honed and readied for one special task, set to it, instead of blundering on by ourselves.

I looked up into the evening sky where the first faint stars began to show. We two were born of Voor, no matter our off-world blood. Creatures—people—like us had once landed here, were caught up in an evil which became a dark blight, an evil which was able to reach out and draw in turn upon some inner quality of my species. Had those refugees indeed been of my own stock or enough like us so that our heritage was a common one?

Only this time our blood had been the victims—except for Illo and me. If the Shadows could move to bend men to their purposes, could not some overwhelming *other* will, seeking ever a weapon against them, have had a hand in what we had done?

"What do we do now—?" I asked it of the sky, and of myself, but Illo answered:

"Nothing. Time will heal. We shall not speak the truth to anyone. It is gone, all of it—that garden place of utter evil in which they fed and spawned, and which I think they needed in order to live—the jewel city where now no one will tramp and pry and seek out secrets we are not meant to handle, use, or know. I am a healer—I shall heal— In time this memory shall fade more and more into a story—"

I sat up, put my fingers to my lips and gave Witol's whistle.

"I do not think we shall forget so easily," I told her. "But, yes, we must keep silent. There will be holdings in the north after the years pass and others find no more trouble. Perhaps the Tangle will fade, it may have been nourished by what lay under it. *Their* peace is locked upon them for all time—" I could still sense a little of what I felt in the city; I hoped I would not forget that healing peace ever. "You are right, this is our secret, we shall remain who we are, and none shall know the difference. After all," I was on my feet now and had stretched wide my arms as if some burden had loosened and fallen, to leave my back unbowed any longer, "what better life can I choose—Voorloper!" I shouted that to the sky in a sudden burst of relief and returning youth, as Witol and his companions came trotting up to the two of us there under the evening sky.

ALL TWELVE TITLES AVAILABLE FROM ACE
$2.25 EACH

☐ 11630 **CONAN, #1**

☐ 11631 **CONAN OF CIMMERIA, #2**

☐ 11632 **CONAN THE FREEBOOTER, #3**

☐ 11633 **CONAN THE WANDERER, #4**

☐ 11634 **CONAN THE ADVENTURER, #5**

☐ 11635 **CONAN THE BUCCANEER, #6**

☐ 11636 **CONAN THE WARRIOR, #7**

☐ 11637 **CONAN THE USURPER, #8**

☐ 11638 **CONAN THE CONQUEROR, #9**

☐ 11639 **CONAN THE AVENGER, #10**

☐ 11640 **CONAN OF AQUILONIA, #11**

☐ 11641 **CONAN OF THE ISLES, #12**

Available wherever paperbacks are sold or use this coupon.

ACE SCIENCE FICTION
P.O. Box 400, Kirkwood, N.Y. 13795

Please send me the titles checked above. I enclose $_____.
Include $1.00 per copy for postage and handling. Send check or
money order only. New York State residents please add sales tax.

NAME_____

ADDRESS_____

CITY_____STATE_____ZIP_____

A-04

ANDRE NORTON